D0345300

CITY
OF
HOOKS AND SCARS

A CITY OF VILLAINS NOVEL

ESTELLE LAURE

CITY
OF
HOOKS AND SCARS

A CITY OF VILLAINS NOVEL

ESTELLE LAURE

DISNEY·HYPERION

LOS ANGELES   NEW YORK

First Edition, April 2022
10 9 8 7 6 5 4 3 2 1
FAC-004510-22049
Printed in the United States of America

This book is set in Adobe Caslon Pro/Adobe
Designed by Phil Buchanan

Library of Congress Cataloging-in-Publication Data
Names: Laure, Estelle, author.
Title: City of hooks and scars / by Estelle Laure.
Description: First edition. • Los Angeles ; New York : Disney Hyperion, 2022. • Series: City of villains ; book 2 • Audience: Ages 14–18. • Audience: Grades 10–12. • Summary: "Teen detective Mary Elizabeth continues to unravel a dark conspiracy that has turned her best friend and boyfriend into villainous monsters—all while battling her own inner demons"—Provided by publisher.
Identifiers: LCCN 2021043702 • ISBN 9781368049399 (hardcover) • ISBN 9781368050333 (paperback) • ISBN 9781368065542 (ebook)
Subjects: CYAC: Villains—Fiction. • Characters in literature—Fiction. • Conspiracies—Fiction. • Magic—Fiction. • LCGFT: Novels.
Classification: LCC PZ7.1.L38 Cih 2022 • DDC [Fic]—dc23
LC record available at https://lccn.loc.gov/2021043702

Reinforced binding
Visit www.DisneyBooks.com

For Laine—
Thank you for letting me bask so long
in the light of your Lainebow.

CITY
OF
HOOKS AND SCARS

A CITY OF VILLAINS NOVEL

ESTELLE LAURE

PROLOGUE

DESIRE AVENUE IS DEAD NOW, NO ONE ON THE streets, all the businesses shuttered and shadowed. Black-and-white shots of James, Ursula, and Mally are slapped across their fronts, warning everyone that the villains have disappeared, no one knows where they are, and to report any sign of them at once.

Use the #fearthevillains hashtag for more information
or to share anything you know, or text 332277.

Mud streaks the sidewalk, left over from the last unexpected storm. All storms are unexpected in the Scar. According to the news reports, there hasn't been more than a light patter of rain here since the weather went on record. That and the flowers in the Ever Garden were all that remained of magic after the Great Death thirteen years ago. Ironic that magic is back and the weather has turned gray and gloomy. I wrestle with my bag of groceries, the baguette I bought my aunt Gia giving me some cover as I pass a Legacy couple in the street carrying five huge packages of toilet paper. They look at me warily as they approach, but I don't think they recognize me.

"Legacy Loyalty," I say.

"Loyalty for life," they say back as they fumble with mountains of plastic.

I finally left the apartment after two days of being trapped inside, the media waiting on the stoop for any signs of me, hoping for a glimpse of James Bartholomew's girlfriend, or for a comment from me since they can't find James. But then today, mercy. Caleb Rothco, aka the Mad Hatter, made a scene at his arraignment. Apparently it was pretty entertaining. It's not quite enough to pull all the focus from the Battle at Miracle Lake and the return of magic, but it's certainly enough to get the reporters off my doorstep and up to Midcity, where the press conference is being held.

It's been two days since everything changed, since my life got ripped away from me without warning and everything got turned on its head. Two days since I cut my boyfriend's hand off with an ax to save him, since my best friend, Ursula, disappeared along with him and vicious Mally Saint, since Wrong Magic showed its face during the battle.

I could have gone with them, but I chose Legacy, the desolate streets of the Scar, and the possibility of finding a way to help them from here. I don't know how yet, but that's exactly what I'm going to do.

ONE

THE PARK AROUND MIRACLE LAKE IS TRANS-
formed. Legacy, those descended from a magical lineage and carry
the Seed mark on their wrists, are everywhere, in satin coats, leather
jackets studded with sequins and silver and gold-colored beads,
decked out in heeled boots and bright hair. They've set up blankets
and lawn chairs on the outskirts of the park, where there are fewer
people, like they've come to watch a parade, a game, a spectacle, a
fun diversion on a Sunday afternoon. They're having snacks and
chatting as I weave among them and finally find a place to stand
out of the way.

The wind blows my hair back from my face, and I pull my hood
tighter around me.

A blast of noise surges from the stage area and we all look up.
#FEAR THE VILLAINS flashes across three enormous screens
like fireworks, along with more obnoxious attention-grabbing
noises. And then there's Mally at the end of the battle when she was
desperate to get away and she magicked herself into a dragon and
tore through the Scar, unleashing fireballs on cops as they tried to
shoot her out of the sky.

The crowd gathers, hushed, some with tears hovering at the

edges of their eyelids, others with their mouths hanging open, stupefied.

There was once magic in the Scar, but even when it was alive and well, it was more the fairies-granting-wishes-type magic than the dragons-snorting-fire-at-you kind. No one has ever seen anything like it.

The spectators cuddle into each other, watching as buildings are set aflame, as officers scatter trying to take cover.

The Legacy around me are afraid, and maybe they should be.

Now Ursula, giant, slimy squid limbs spilling out everywhere, towers over the city. Her yellow eyes shine spotlights into the streets as she swipes at anything she can reach. She doesn't do much damage, but I don't think anyone notices that. She is monstrous for sure, gone full kaiju.

As the scene changes to the door in front of Wonderland, the bar where I spend so much of my time, I know what's coming next and my lungs empty out, squashed. I clench my fists and jaw, and wait.

The sound of club music bounces out onto the street. People pass by in groups wearing costumes, commemorating the death of magic, honoring our families and all we have lost, as we do every year.

"We're at Wonderland! We're actually in the Scar!" a girl squeals, then says, "Get in the frame! We need evidence."

Another girl trots into view, adjusting her hair, just as, behind her, a guy with red hair and black-and-white-checkered shoes comes out of Wonderland. He reaches into his pocket and then stops, completely still, like someone hit pause on him.

The girl who's filming her friend says, "What the hell?"

And then she realizes it's not just him who's frozen, it's not just the guy outside of Wonderland reaching into his pocket for his phone or whatever. It's happening *inside* Wonderland, too. The girl filming zooms in on the dance floor and the bar. Everyone is completely still, not moving, not even *breathing*. The music beats on, but they're immobilized.

I buckle, then will myself to keep it together.

"Tracy," the girl filming says, voice shaking. "Tracy, look!"

Her friend, a girl with voluminous black hair and too much lip gloss, lets out a shriek and says, "Oh, holy mother," just as James comes barreling through the doors holding a girl dressed all in black, who's clinging to him like he's the only thing keeping her from death.

He is.

The girl is me.

James glares up and down the street, eyes on fire, then, in two bounds, leaps over a car, denting it as he goes, and takes off between two high-rise buildings, disappearing from sight. Once we're gone, the people inside Wonderland all flop to the floor at once. So does the guy, the bouncer who was just outside. He collides with the wall. The girl holding the phone screams long and hard.

A message flashes across the screen:

#fearthevillains
Text 332277 with information

I breathe again now that the clip is done, I try to tamp down the surge of emotion that rips through me. I miss James so much, even with his eyes glowing like that, with him sweaty and out of control. I assume the Monarch police have an eye on me, so I haven't gone to all the places I think he might be, but even if I did, I wouldn't find him. James Bartholomew is not in the Scar, but he would never leave it. How can both things be true?

Before the screen goes black again, a guy with a mop of blond hair runs out onto the stage, taps the mic, then runs back offstage left. The crowd rumbles before ripping into applause as two uniformed police officers and Mayor Triton sidle across the stage. Triton looks sturdy, tanklike, if a little soft in the middle. She never comes to the Scar. I've personally never taken much interest in her. Crime was my thing, which is why I applied for an internship with the Monarch City Police while I was still in high school. Politicians have always seemed a combination of uninteresting and pathetic, whereas law enforcement like Chief Ito had real power to effect change, to save lives and put criminals behind bars. That's where I envisioned myself. I didn't realize that Chief Ito was a politician, too, and just as pathetic, just as much of a liar as the rest of them. Worse, even, because Chief Ito is Legacy. She has the Seed mark. She should remember where she came from. She is one of us.

I watch Mayor Triton with renewed interest now, and apparently I'm not the only one. All the Legacy around me are freaking out like she's a rock star.

The mayor puts her hands on the lectern and stares solemnly outward, waiting for the perfect moment to begin. "Citizens of the Scar," she says, "valued members of the Legacy community, I stand before you because the city of Monarch faces unprecedented times. We occupy a special pocket on this planet. We have always taken this job seriously and reverentially. Even after the Great Death, we have sought to preserve our history, and many of us have hoped for magic's return."

There's a murmur of agreement, and the woman beside me hoots and holds up a sign that reads MAGICALISTS AGAINST THE VILLAINS in jagged crimson paint.

"While many of us hoped the Scar would reassume its former glory, we never imagined that the return of magic would bring with it such dark tidings." The mayor raises her hands theatrically and shakes her head. "The very sky has turned against us." She pauses. "Magic has indeed returned as we have all hoped for so long. But not as the bright and loving force for good it once was. It has returned as evil."

Behind her the two-story images appear again: James with a new, shiny hook, all covered in tattoos; Mally with her sharp, dangerous horns; and Ursula with her seeking, oil-slick tentacles. All three of them are sneering, menacing, frothing at the mouth. They look nothing like the people I love. It's easy to imagine they're evil villains instead of regular kids who ended up on the wrong end of someone's plan. But they *are* kids.

"Since the Battle at Miracle Lake, life as we know it in the Scar has changed, and change it must," the mayor goes on, tapping the lectern to emphasize her words. "If this were an isolated event and we could trust these villains were gone for good, we would not continue to fear the worst. But we know this is not the case. We fear the villains are only at the beginning of a violent spree, and because they have power we cannot compete with, they will continue to use it to wreak havoc on the Scar and its citizens. They are cowards, so they hide, but nevertheless, they are unpredictable and extremely dangerous." Mayor Triton sighs, pauses, gathers herself. "It is with the heaviest of hearts that I share the tragic news that in the last three days, two of the Scar's precious Legacy children have disappeared without a trace."

Another ripple of alarm threads through the crowd. A few cries emerge. Mayor Triton nods.

"With the help of the Monarch police, we have been able to determine that the chilcren have been taken by the villains, villains we now know mean to do us harm. There have also been reports of various sightings, which is how we know James Bartholomew now wears a hook for a hand, and we are relying on you for more information. No tip is too small. We need your help to bring the villains in and get them under control."

"Kill them!" someone shouts.

There are howls of agreement, and the crowd gets loud and pushy. Cameras snap from all sides. The mayor settles everyone down with a few nods.

"I want to assure all of you that we are doing everything we can. Along with our stellar chief of police, who is frankly the best in the country, maybe the world, we will not rest until we track down the villains, and I have no doubt we will be successful in bringing them to justice."

The crowd cheers.

I spot Gia's friends off to the side, decorated in beads and swaddled in bright clothes, collectively holding up a sheet that says NATURALISTS FOR PEACE! I steal out of their line of vision.

"This evening," the mayor goes on, "I am introducing a series of emergency initiatives that will help us navigate this time, and I seek your full cooperation. I trust that you understand the gravity of what lies ahead." She pauses, waiting for everyone's full attention. "Until further notice, the Scar will observe a nine p.m. curfew, and I encourage all citizens to go to work, and then go home. Keep your children off the streets. Do not linger outside your homes. Do not stay out unnecessarily after dark."

There are a few murmurs, but most stay silent. I get what she's trying to do by making everyone feel safe, but also, I know it's not going to help anything. Beatrix Lindl disappeared two days ago, right from her apartment. I know because Cindy, who's part of Gia's Naturalist group, is her aunt. Beatrix, who has cerebral palsy, was brushing her teeth when her dad heard a thump. She had fallen before, so he thought it had happened again and rushed into the bathroom and found her toothbrush in the sink with the water running and no sign of Beatrix anywhere. No sign of anything except a single line of damage to the wall next to the sink. Damage that might come from a hook. And Beatrix was gone.

Poof. Vanished.

But yeah. By all means stay huddled in your house. That'll keep you and your kids safe.

The mayor goes on. "We will also be setting up a special task force, which we have named the Watch. Composed of Legacy as well as Monarch City Police, their mission is threefold: One, they will protect; two, they will bring the villains to justice; and three, they will be collecting information about illegal magic and cracking down on it with the full force of the new emergency laws we have put in place."

There are some sounds of protest, but they're minimal.

"Magic has always been a source of pride for Monarch and especially, of course, for the Scar, but this is not the magic we know and love. It's an evil perversion. I know it won't be easy, that it's asking so much of you when you are already cold and afraid and facing a vast unknown, but if you see *any* signs of magic being practiced, we ask you to report to the Watch by texting three-three-two-two-seven-seven. This is a sacred duty and is the only way to keep Legacy safe."

The crowd goes wild. People jump up and down.

I can't believe what I'm seeing. They're buying this.

I don't understand all the details of this situation yet, but I know my friends are victims, not villains, and no amount of spin is going to convince me of anything different. People are afraid, and yes, the fact that kids are disappearing is unsettling for sure, but it doesn't make any sense that Kyle Attenborough isn't anywhere in this conversation. He's the one who kidnapped my friends and experimented on them, and he's the one who found a way to bring whatever this magic is to the Scar. He considered Legacy kids expendable, and he used them to try to find a marketable form of magic. The police and the mayor have to know this. I saw Kyle get arrested the night of the battle.

Not a single mention of him or his son, Lucas. No mention of the lab where the so-called villains were being held in cages, either? It doesn't make sense. Except Kyle Attenborough has money, enough to buy whoever he wants. My friends are scapegoats while Kyle Attenborough is somewhere in the Narrows sitting on a golden throne.

I hug myself and look around. Maybe I should have gone with them after all. And what's going to happen when they're found? I picture them hanging from this same stage, people all around jeering. They've forgotten James and Mally and Urs are Legacy. They belong to the Scar.

"I heard since James Bartholomew has a hook for a hand now," says a boy with sloppy bangs and a nose ring, "he makes people walk the plank and wears a patch over one eye."

"Well, I heard Ursula the sea monster steals people's essences and keeps them in some kind of prison in the ocean. It's called the Garden of Poor Unfortunate Souls or something. Terrible. Just awful," says a woman next to him.

"Where are you hearing this?" I ask the boy.

"Huh?" he says.

"I said, where are you hearing these rumors? The plank, the souls . . . all of it." My heart is racing, not because I think he's lying but because it sounds like what he says could be true, and if it is, then someone, somewhere knows where they are.

"Hey," the woman says, hiking up her dress, which is too big and falling down over her shoulders. "I know you. You're Captain Crook's girlfriend."

"Hell yeah you are. Hey!" the boy yells. "James Bartholomew's girl is over here harassing me!"

I narrow my eyes at him, wishing I could still do any kind of useful magic, and then look away and dash deeper into the crowd, closer to the front. That was not intelligent. Chief Ito needs to think I'm an annoying little gnat who's out of her hair once and for all.

You think approaching that little weevil was unintelligent? What was unintelligent was not snapping his neck. One hard crank would have done it. Would have been as refreshing as a cold plunge.

Oh good. Great. Excellent. She's back. The voice that's been in my head since the night of the battle, the only thing left of the reaction I had to the magic Lucas forced in me. She sounds like me, but . . . mean. Like, really mean.

And She won't shut up. I really wish I'd been left with something more useful. Mally had some sort of magical staff. Where's mine?

As though She's punishing me for thinking such thoughts, a pulse throbs in my temples and I remember the ax coming down hard on James's wrist. She's not wrong about how good it felt, how *final.* And now he might have cold metal to replace his overheated flesh? What else would he do? Wear a prosthetic? That's not really his style.

You should join James, She says, and my skin curdles. *Look at these losers. Why did you choose them over him?* The voice is raspy and slow.

Like I said, She won't shut up.

I weave my way out of the crowd, start to make my way home to Gia, when a man with a beard and rabid eyes waves a sign in my face. OFF WITH THEIR HEADS! it reads. I blink hard, and when I look again, the sign reads WHAT'S GOING ON IN THEIR HEADS?

The last time I saw James, Urs, and Mally, we stood on a darkened street with James bleeding out on the pavement and Mally swanning around impatiently. They asked me to go with them, but just then, I couldn't conceive of it. I wasn't thinking of where we might go or what that could mean for any of us. I was only thinking it wouldn't be here, and that it would mean choosing not to be inside the system anymore. I was still imagining a future as a detective, myself as the lone arbiter of justice, a necessary piece of the Scar's complicated clockwork. I imagined, as much as I could process in the few seconds I had, that if I went with them, I would be tipping the balances of the Scar so far into chaos it would never be able to right itself again.

I thought I was that important.

And I thought about Gia, leaving her behind, being a fugitive. What that would do to her. There would have to be no hope left for me to abandon her like that. But I should have asked where they were going, when they would be back. We should have made a meeting place and time. I couldn't have predicted how maddening it would be to be left alone, everything gone south without any of them.

It hurts.

And while I wasn't given nearly as much of the Wrong Magic as them, it's still inside me, too, affecting me.

I don't know what you're complaining about, She says just as I push myself free of the crowd and head for the back entrance to my building. *Now you're not so all alone. You have* me!

But I don't want *Her.* I want James. I want Ursula. And I want them back the way they were before they were stolen from me. I need to do two things: find them and find some sort of cure. Otherwise it's only a matter of time before they all end up swinging in the wind.

I'm not going to let that happen.

As the frenzy builds behind me, Legacy bashing into each other, howling along with the noise coming off the stage, I know exactly where to start undoing this knot.

Monarch High.

TWO

AS SOON AS I SEE MONARCH HIGH TOWERING IN front of me Monday morning, I know I'm not at all as strong as I thought I was. As in, I'm about to crumble inside and possibly go fetal on this very green, very pretty lawn, and that would not be good. It's one thing to sneak into a rally and then sneak out again, basically undetected. It's another thing entirely to be here at Monarch High with everyone who knows and loathes me squished into one building, especially now that they've got posters of James, Mally, and Urs everywhere they can find a free surface.

WELCOME BACK, MONARCH HIGH! The marquee flashes an optimistic rainbow, and underneath: PLEASE OBSERVE ALL THE RULES!

I should turn back, go home, get into bed, and never leave again. I don't want to have to face them, the kids at school, to answer their questions, deal with their judgments. James and Urs are gone, and everyone in this school knows I was with them the night of the battle. We never really flew under the radar to begin with, and now there'll be a spotlight on me. I'll come back tomorrow, try again another day.

What do you want? To be a sniveling loser or . . .

The voice again. Always there to comment on what I do.

Though She may have a point.

What do I want?

"James," I whisper. I feel the truth in my gut, but it's followed by the questions that have been plaguing me. Is he safe? If so, is he angry? If so, can he forgive me? If so, will he ever want to see me again? If so, can he believe that I am still loyal to him? If so, will he accept my apology?

If so, can we be saved?

Only one way to find out.

Well then.

One foot in front of the other, coward.

I'm prepared for Monarch High—which was a pit of despair and destruction cloaked in Caramel Frappuccinos way before the Battle of Miracle Lake—to feel even more awkward and unhinged than it did five days ago, but I still lurch to a stop when I see what's actually going on here.

Thanks to the Scar Restoration Initiative, the circular driveway is landscaped with tulips and kelly-green grass, lined with peony clusters bursting with flowers of plush purples and pinks. The fountain at its center still spits water from the mouth of a pale blue sea dragon. All of that is the same as before. Same attempt to prettify all the fights and issues bubbling over around here. But the vehicle lane, usually peppered with school buses and limos dropping off Narrows kids, is now lined entirely with a fleet of white SUVs, each one rectangular in shape, identical and unmarked, with tinted windows. Unidentifiable as Narrows or Legacy, people in gray suits stand at attention outside the vehicles, line the stairs up to the main doors, and are posted on either side.

The Watch.

They must be. Welp, they are definitely watching.

I search for familiar faces but find none, not Smee or the Lost Boys. There isn't even any sign of Flora or Fauna or Merryweather, at least not that I can see from here. I guess it's not surprising the Lost Boys wouldn't be here. They only came to school because James made them, told them it was important to get a good education, and now that he's gone, I'm sure they've been up all night gaming and are getting settled in for a nice day of snoozing.

And ... the press. Camera crews are parked around the periphery, and journalists in raincoats are speaking into microphones. They don't have much of a chance of getting anywhere near the school with the Watch in their way, so I guess that's good. One less thing to worry about.

Bold.

Be bold.

What kind of life do you want?

I mount the stairs as the student body shuffles closer to the door.

Almost everyone in the line to get into the building has some sort of coat on, hoods and hats covering their heads, thick scarves wrapped around their necks. The Scar is usually bright colors, tan limbs, wild makeup, over-the-top jewelry. This sea of neutral outerwear is just plain weird.

Then I see him, hovering in an alcove, looking directly at me: Lucas Attenborough. I almost don't recognize him. He's wearing jeans and lace-ups with a loose button-down instead of his usual khakis-with-a-tucked-in-shirt-and-loafers uniform. Looks like the hood on my sweatshirt isn't doing much to conceal me. Not when it comes to Lucas. He always has been annoyingly observant. He meets my eyes, nods at me, and dares to quirk the corner of his mouth into a smile.

He smiled at me after everything.

If James were here, he would knock him into the next school year.

But he's not.

Only I am.

I raise my chin, will him to feel my hatred and for it to eat him from the inside out. I remember how I broke glass with my mind the night of the battle, how I made it disappear. I haven't been able to muster anything fabulous or powerful since, but I wonder if I'm angry enough now to break Lucas in half or make him disappear. That would really perk up my day. I try to beam destruction at him, but nothing happens. I fizzle immediately.

Three days ago, Lucas Attenborough knocked me unconscious, kidnapped me, drugged me, and shot me up with his Wrong Magic. I want Lucas to know I'm not afraid of him or his dad, even though it's not entirely true.

He did take me against my will, lock me up, and restrain me. That is not an easy thing to forget.

He seems to understand, and only when I have won the staring contest do I begin to wonder what Lucas, Prince of the Narrows, is doing outside by himself. In all the time I've known Lucas Attenborough I've never seen him alone, especially not at school. Here, he is worshiped or loathed. Never ignored.

He pulls out his phone, pretending to be busy. I shuffle forward.

"Hood down." The man from the Watch points at my head.

"What? Why?"

This guy's not much older than me, maybe five years at most. He's well built and wearing a watch that covers his wrist, so I can't see whether or not he has a Seed mark. He thrusts a piece of paper in my hand. "No hats." He taps the paper. "It's Legacy Pride Wear. Please review the rules."

I glance at the damp paper.

USE OF THE WORD *MAGIC* IS PROHIBITED UNTIL FURTHER NOTICE.

MENTION OF AFFILIATIONS, SUCH AS MAGICALIST, AMAGICALIST,

AND NATURALIST, ARE PROHIBITED.

USE OF THE TERM *NARROWS* IS PROHIBITED.

USE OF THE TERM *LEGACY* IS PROHIBITED.

LEGACY PRIDE IS NOT PERMITTED ON CAMPUS,

INCLUDING HATS, HOODS, AND WIGS.

THE NEW SCHOOL MOTTO IS "ALL FOR ONE AND ONE FOR ALL"

AND MUST BE RECITED UPON REQUEST.

"How is a hoodie an example of Legacy Pride?"

"Use of the term 'legacy' is against the rules. Move along."

I'd give a couple of fingernails to see Mally incinerate this flyer with that fancy new staff of hers.

He moves to let me through and goes on to the next person, repeating his instructions robotically.

Once inside, things look more normal. A few members of the Watch line the halls, but it's not an overwhelming presence. The coffee cart is still in full effect with a line going most of the way out the door. The floor is squeaky and sludgy from rainy shoes, and the place smells a little like mothballs, but it's warm and well lit and filled with nervous chatter. I find my way into the coffee line and am about to have a better look at the sheet of paper in my hands when I feel the energy around me begin to shift.

The conversation drops. Heads turn in my direction. I curse myself for not thinking this through better, doing a dry run of how I was going to handle the attention. Dropping to the floor and playing possum probably isn't any more of an option than thrashing about murderously. Ursula would know what to do. Even James would make this work to his advantage. Mally would just set everyone on fire.

"Is it true you cut off James's hand?" asks a girl I vaguely recognize. I consider yanking her septum ring out of her nose. "Was it gross?" she asks. "Was it literally so gross?"

"I heard you have powers. Is that why you won't talk to the news? Are they going to arrest you? We aren't even allowed to say the M-word anymore. Did you know that?" a boy asks.

The M-word?

"If you all would have listened to the Amagicalists in the first place, this never would have happened," spits Justin, leader of the Amagicalist Youth Society. "The obsession with magic is behind every bad thing that's ever happened in the Scar. We don't need that here. We need to learn to rely on ourselves."

"Where'd you hear that?" the first girl snaps. "You get that from your Amagicalist manual, aka the world's most boring piece of reading *ever*?"

"You guys!" yet another girl says. "We are not supposed to use those words. We're going to be in trouble."

I don't know if it's just in my head or what, but it feels like they all take a step forward at once. "I need to find Morgana," I say, while I have their attention. "She's a ninth grader?"

"You mean Morgana, *Ursula's sister*? Like anyone doesn't know who she is," the girl says.

She seriously needs to check her tone, and I'm about to tell her so when a voice flutters through the commons. "You're looking for me?"

There's a ripple of motion as the waves part. Morgie steps through the portal of humans, and I have to steady myself. Dressed in a strapless black minidress with her long blond hair straightened to razor points, she looks like a completely different person than the last time I saw her. It's like she's aged years in the last week, gone from little girl to almost woman. There's that . . . and she looks so much like Ursula. She's thinner, maybe, her face eggier, but she's done her makeup just like Urs: blue eye shadow, pulled her eyeliner out past her lids, done her lips in a dramatic crimson. Their faces are more similar than I ever noticed before. She has fake lashes and long red nails just like Urs, and suddenly I'm pretty sure I'm not going to be able to survive another minute without Ursula and her amazing laugh.

The halls used to echo with it.

She used to make the halls quake.

"Morgie," I manage.

"I'm going by 'Morgana' now," she says coldly, then steps forward and gives me a kiss on the cheek. "Hello, Mary Elizabeth."

That's when I realize she's not alone, that she's flanked by several girls dressed in black, their hair in updos and black bows, and chokers around their necks.

"Are you going to introduce me to your friends?" I ask.

"Tabitha, Lee, Sarah. No need to remember their names." She tilts her head. "Mary, Mary, quite contrary," she says. "Girls, you know Mary, right? Hatchet Mary?"

Oh cool. I have a nickname. I see the blade slicing through the sinew of James's wrist and blink hard to bring myself back to the hall.

The girls nod and say hi, but they keep glancing at Morgie like they're waiting for instructions.

"Can we talk?" I pull Morgie away from the crowd toward the lockers and give the girls a look to let them know they'd better stay put.

"I have to go to class," she says, wrenching herself free.

I check the clock over Morgie's head. "We still have five minutes before the bell."

She folds her arms across her chest. "Okay, then."

"I want to say I'm sorry."

She raises an eyebrow. "Oh yeah? What do you have to be sorry for?"

"I've been a real toad not reaching out to you. I should have come to see you after the battle and everything that happened with Urs. I should have been thinking about you. It must have all been so scary."

"And Ma."

"Ma?"

"You should have been thinking about my ma, too. There's two of us who got left behind."

"Yeah. And your ma. I haven't been there for you the way Urs would want me to be. With her disappearing, you not knowing if she was alive, and now this. It's really a lot."

"Yeah, it is." She taps her long nails on her patent-leather clutch purse. "You've been a really bad friend, Mary. Urs would be so mad at you."

I bristle. I may not have been there for them the way I should have, but it's not like it's been easy for me, either. I've barely been able to leave my house. I haven't been to see the Lost Boys, either. And guess what? No one's checked on me. No one has come to see how I've been doing. It's just been Auntie G and me, staring at the TV, drinking coffee, and wrapping up makeup and skin products to ship overseas.

Now's not the time to be petty and have unrealistic expectations. We should be there and take care of each other. We can do better, starting now.

I mean to tell Morgie all this, but I wait a beat too long, and before I can begin, she leans into one hip in a bad imitation of her sister and grins.

"Luckily, we don't need you," she says. "I can take care of both of us."

"Oh yeah?"

"Yeah. Urs left me a present." She reaches into her backpack and pulls out a beat-up black book I recognize instantly. I've seen it hundreds of times . . . in Ursula's hands. This book is where Urs kept an analog record of the people at school who owed her favors who had made a deal with her, or who were indebted to her in some way. I always saw it for what it was: Ursula's way of making sure the world owed her too much to take what was hers or hurt her any more than it already had. And now Morgie has picked up where Urs left off.

Godmothers, help us all.

If Ursula could have kept Morgana from ever feeling the need to go follow in her footsteps, she would have. I don't believe Ursula left her anything that would invite her into this. Not on purpose.

"And by *left* do you mean you went into her room, into her things, and took it?"

Morgie smirks. "What difference does it make? She's gone. The book is mine now and everyone knows it. That's all that matters."

A headache is forming at my temples. "You're going to find really quickly that being your sister isn't as glamorous as you think."

Her arrogance falters, but only for a second. She narrows her eyes. "What do you want, Mary? I know you weren't looking for me so you could apologize, so let's not play games."

"I do need something from you."

"Mm-hmm." She flips to a new page in the notebook, pulls a pen from her bag.

"I was hoping you could tell me if you've seen Urs since the night of the battle? In person, I mean," I say. "Gotten any texts? Calls? Do you know where she is?"

Morgie looks up from the notebook and gives me a once-over.

"What if I *have* seen her?" Morgie says. "What's it worth to you?"

I'm so shocked I can't even speak. She lets out a loud giggle. "I'm just kidding!" She slaps my arm and closes the book. "I don't know where she is. She came in and out a few times, always while we were sleeping, got the rug so wet we had to have it pulled up because the mildew was making Ma sick. I don't even think she came for us. I think she was looking for something."

I think of Urs's phone, the one Bella and I broke into that had all that information about her beef with Caleb Rothco, the Mad Hatter, on it. Her little black book has nothing on that SIM card.

"You're absolutely sure you don't know where she is?" I press. "I just need to talk to her."

"Let's say I know exactly where she is. What will you do if I tell you? Aren't you a cop?"

"Not anymore. I don't have anything to do with them." I look at her seriously. "I'll try to get her back here. I'll make everything the way it was."

Morgie takes a step toward me. We're so close I can feel her breath on my chin.

"Let me tell you a couple of things," she says. "One, I'm not afraid of you."

"I'm not trying to scare you," I say. "I want to help you get things back to normal."

She holds up a hand. "Save it, Scary Mary."

A new crowd of kids is gathering, pretending to talk while sucking on sweet coffees.

"Two," she says, "I don't want it to go back to the way it was. Urs doesn't care about us any more than you do. Tromping everywhere like some overgrown jellyfish. It's embarrassing. Didn't even think about how it would affect us. She's always been selfish, and now she's worse than ever. I wish she had been dead, like they were saying before the battle. It would all be so much easier."

"You don't mean that—"

"I do mean it. Ma and I wouldn't take her back if she did dare to show her face around here. And three, unless you're here to offer me a shot of some of that sweet, sweet *magic* the others got, I'm not interested."

She smiles and shows me all her teeth as a wave of intrigue ripples through the crowd.

I shiver. Urs, who is warm and fun loving if a little mischievous every now and then, has never made me feel this way, like something serpentine is coiled and waiting to strike.

Morgie leans over and pulls me into a hug, digs her fingers into my shoulders. "If you ever find it—the magic, I mean—I'll be happy to make a deal. And these days, I could be just the ally you need."

"Morgie, what happened to you?" I say into her neck, even though I already know. This is what happens when you're left underwater one too many times to claw yourself to the surface.

She pulls away, leaving a musky, slightly animal scent in her wake that makes me want to gag.

"I became myself," she answers. "Jealous?"

"Jealous? No, I'm not jealous. Definitely not of you." She gives me a pitying glare, just as the bell rings and the hall erupts into a flurry of activity.

She flips her hair and spares me one more glance. "If you ask me, your plan is pretty lacking. You can't bring Ursula and James back here the way they are. You'd have to cure them. And how do you plan to do that before the Watch gets to them? Let them go. It's for the best."

That hits me hard. She's absolutely right, and I never thought of it until now. I mean, obviously we would need a plan, a way to bring them back safely, but we don't just need a plan . . . we need an antidote, a cure for the Wrong Magic. That's the answer.

Even though I have no idea how I'm going to get my hands on one, I kind of want to kiss Morgie right now for thinking of it. But before I can, she says, "Also, did you ever ask yourself why Ursula and James haven't gotten in touch with you? Maybe it's because they like it better without you around, always there to tell them when they're being too bad for your taste. Maybe they've been waiting years to get rid of you." Her words sting. "If you see my sister, tell her not to come home. Tell her she's not wanted anymore. Come on, girls."

She saunters down the hall, with her friends trailing behind her.

I make it through my econ class (everything is bad, the world is doomed, and the economy is basically fake) trying not to obsess over the things Morgie said to me, and then I drift back out into the hallway. My presence is still drawing attention, and yes, I had to sit all the way in the back with Stone to avoid being gawked at, but it's getting better. This will be like exposure therapy, which is what my therapist, Dr. Tink, theorized was essentially what I was doing by being on the police force in the first place. Being a cop meant facing my fear of sociopathic criminals and murderers, people whose only purpose was to hurt others, like the man who had robbed my family of their lives. This will be like that, but with teenagers instead of homicide.

After class, Katy is leaning against my locker. Katy of the Narrows. Katy of the sharp bob and the pointed nose and the triangular pointy beige flats. Katy, who is normally glued to Lucas Attenborough's side. Right now there's no sign of him. Maybe they're not BFFs anymore.

Sigh.

I had almost expunged her from my memory. Almost.

Before I reach Katy, which I have to do since she's actually blocking the path to my locker and therefore my math tablet, Dreena slides up next to me. "Mary, I'm so happy you're here. I thought maybe you wouldn't want to show your face or something, but I also knew you were brave, and I just want you to know if you need somewhere to sit at lunch . . . since your friends are . . . well . . . We've got you covered."

I don't want to take my eyes off Katy, but at the mention of a *we*, I look behind me to find we're being trailed by at least five of Dreena's Academic Excellence Council members. These are the girls who are always protesting something, meeting to work on their essays, trying to make a difference in the Scar. They are a faithful army.

"Thanks, Dreena. I have to deal with something right now, okay?" I say. "But I'll definitely look for you later."

Dreena eyes Katy. "Isn't that your locker?"

"Yeah, it is," I say. "Why is Katy standing in front of it?" she asks.

"I'll see you, okay?"

"Okay, yeah . . . I'll see you at lunch."

"OMG," Katy says as I approach, glancing up from her phone. "I had to see it with my own two eyes."

I don't like her, but I want to keep it chill.

"I can't believe you'd come back here after making a total fool of yourself with your trashy friends all over town," Katy says, "I know you were having a mental breakdown or whatever. I just want to make sure you're aware that I know you're unstable. Everyone in the Scar is waiting for you to screw up, which you will. Like I always say, trash will be trash." She sniffs, then meets my eyes and smiles. "And you *are* trash, Mary Elizabeth. Now that your little friends are gone, there's no one here to protect you, so watch your back."

I don't exactly see what happens next so much as I feel it. Dreena whips by me in a blur. I thought she had gone on down the hall, but her black hair is flailing about wildly as she sends out a warrior cry and goes straight for Katy's neck with arms outstretched.

"Don't talk to Mary like that!" Dreena screams, and her friends follow closely behind as Narrows pop out from everywhere and join the fray.

"No, Dreena, no!" I yell, but she's at the bottom of a dog pile now, so I start pulling bodies from the top.

My stomach lurches when I see Lucas running toward us. I expect to feel a hit as he lands a punch to the side of my face or something, but he doesn't do that. Instead he goes for his Narrows crew and begins pulling them off the Legacy kids. He must be trying to get to Katy, who has been knocked onto her back, struggling as Dreena, who is far more badass than I ever would have imagined, doesn't let her budge and punches at Katy's perfect, expensive nose.

I'm trying to get one of Dreena's friends to safety when each of my arms is grabbed. I see gray sleeves as I'm pulled to my feet. Lucas looks up as multiple members of the Watch descend to control the crowd.

"Are you okay?" he yells.

"Go suck an—"

"No swearing. Against the rules," one of the Watch says.

"Where are you taking her?" Lucas says.

They don't answer.

I try to murder him with my eyeballs again. "Stop acting concerned!" I yell. "Literally everything is your fault."

Before he can answer, I'm pivoted around to face the empty part of the hall. The Watch is being unnecessarily assertive. I glance down at the hand clamped on to my wrist.

"You're Legacy?" I ask.

"We do not refer to Legacy. Against the rules." The female voice is pulled tight as a rubber band.

"Where are you taking me?" I demand as I struggle.

"Principal's office," another female voice says. "Your presence has been requested by Principal Iago."

"Iago's the principal?" I say, still squirming. "Fairy boots, we're done for."

"Miss Heart," Iago says.

While I've always kind of liked Mr. Iago, there's no doubt he's a sniveling panderer. It's only that he's the kind of sniveling panderer that usually leaves students alone, so he doesn't hurt anyone.

He looks me over like he's checking me for weapons. "Please sit."

"I'd rather stand."

"Sit," he says, like I'm a dog.

I don't. The two women flanking me put pressure on my shoulders until I sink into the chair.

"Thank you, that will be all," he says to the Watch. "Can you help round up the rest of the kids who were involved in the fight? Take them all to the cafeteria. I'll meet you there in a few minutes."

The Watch nod and leave the door cracked. I catch a glimpse of Ms. Cruz, the principal's assistant. She's keeping an eye on us, and I feel a little safer knowing that there's a witness.

"Come on, Mary," the principal says when the quiet has settled in the room. "We can be friends."

I don't respond. I'm fuming but also looking around this office with some curiosity. Iago is Legacy, but there's no sign of it anywhere. In fact, there's no personality whatsoever, only a big sign that says TEAMWORK MAKES THE DREAM WORK in irritating pastels.

"What happened to Principal Brown?" I ask.

"Actually," he says, "there were some changes made at the Department of Education and Ms. Brown chose not to continue in her capacity as Monarch High's leader. They've given the position to me." He sits up a little taller and watches me with beady brown eyes, his hair greasy, nose sweating.

Principal Brown must have gotten edged out. I know the Department of Education accused Monarch High of teaching a biased curriculum that favored Legacy, and since more and more Narrows have been moving in, maybe it got heated enough that Brown couldn't deal anymore. She was a nice lady who only accepted Narrows money because it was either that or let the whole school get shut down. "Congratulations?"

"Thank you. And how are you, Miss Heart?" he asks.

"Dandy," I say, and kick my feet up onto the desk.

He eyes them but doesn't complain.

"I'm so pleased to hear that. We were all so worried about you, all the teachers, everyone really. But I think there's been a little miscommunication. I tried to reach you over the weekend."

You and everyone else, I think. I've gotten interview requests from every news outlet—print and television—death threats, and apparently there's some sort of online fan club for the villains that's been calling me a *lot*.

"You are the only one from the Battle of Miracle Lake who isn't on the wanted list, so I know this won't seem fair to you, but . . ." he says.

"But what?"

"Well, how shall I put this? You're a symbol of power, like it or not."

I start to protest.

"No, no," he says. "Then of course there's the whole chopping off of James's hand. . . . You're nothing short of a celebrity around here, you know? Loved or reviled, nothing in between. We do not need that sort of polarity right now, not when we're trying to unify." He clasps his hands in a show of togetherness.

"This is high school," I say. "They'll be bored of this in a couple of days."

"Add to that the fact that we've had yet another student Vanish this morning. That makes five of Monarch's children, with four total disappearances over the weekend. And so I don't think this is the type of thing that will fade after a couple of days. We're talking about the return of the M-word, missing children, and maniacs on the loose."

He whispers the last bit, and I roll my eyes.

"Look at what just happened in the hall. Perfect case in point. Your presence is"—he looks upward, as though searching for the right words—"agitating."

"Agitating," I repeat.

"What I'm saying is that if you were to be here, you'd be expected to obey all rules, not to draw attention to yourself, and to demonstrate the highest levels of discretion and respect for the systems we have in place."

"Okay, I can do that."

"You see, you say that now. . . ."

"I will."

"Miss Heart, you might have the best of intentions, but I don't think so."

"Quite frankly," he continues, "this place is being held together by a thread and a prayer. I think it's best if you do your assigned work from home until the villains have been brought to justice and our children have been returned. Things can only be good here at Monarch High if everyone follows the rules. All for one and—"

"One for all," I finish.

"Exactly. I don't see how I can foster that culture when you are the fulcrum of the Scar's most recent disaster, a disaster that appears to be in the process of unfolding, perhaps even as we speak." He clears his throat and leans back. "The point is, Miss Heart, if you leave now and agree to my terms, I see no need to bring your aunt into all this. I'll give you some paperwork for her to sign, and you can simply go home. No need to tell her about this morning's incident."

At the mention of my aunt, I remove my feet from his desk and sit up.

Gia's sleeping right now, and she's been so stressed out I can just imagine what getting called into the school because of a huge fight would do to her.

"We've accepted that things are changing," he says kindly. "We know the villains are out there."

"They aren't villains."

"Really? How do you explain a giant dragon?" he says. "And a sea monster? A boy who can stop time and render an entire population defenseless? That's not *our* kind of sparkle, is it?" He shakes his head. "They aren't your friends anymore, just a couple of harmless teens with a penchant for a little trouble. They *are* dangerous. They *are* a threat." He pauses. "No, no. We may never truly understand what happened, but we have to go on, and I can only do that if the students are on board. *All* the students. They need to *believe* in what we're trying to do here."

"Which is what?"

"Establish order," he says. "They have to believe their leaders are capable of keeping them safe. Footage shows you were not directly involved in the fight, so I can let you go. Dreena Quintanilla, on the other hand . . ." He refocuses on me. "I don't know what came over her, but you were clearly in the middle of it, and I have a huge mess to deal with now. Please go home. Your teachers will be in touch with you about how you can get your homework done. We'll make sure you finish up and graduate on time."

"Wait, so I can't come back here *ever*?"

"Now, now, let's not get ahead of ourselves. You graduate in June, and it's only November. We have months to go and so much could happen. If the villains are caught, we can revisit the idea of you coming back in person, but until then I think it's best for everyone concerned if we take a little time to adjust to this new normal."

It's not like I love it here, but now I have no internship. No friends. No boyfriend. No school.

Wonderful.

You see, says the voice in my head. *Are you beginning to understand? You aren't wanted here anymore.*

Iago gets up and comes around his desk.

"I know this can't be easy for you. Since the day you walked through those doors hand in hand with James Bartholomew, always with Ursula nearby, I've seen how much they mean to you. I know what you've lost. But can you understand that I'm trying to bring this school together? It's an almost-impossible task, and I don't think I can do it with you here. I'm so sorry."

"Yeah." I nod, aching for the feel of James's arm around my shoulder, to be sheltered by him, and protected by Ursula, much as I wanted to prove I didn't need protection from her. I just want to feel like I'm part of something again. I want my people back.

"All for one," I say, not thinking of the school at all.

Iago pats my hand. "One for all."

THREE

"MORNING," GIA SINGSONGS. SHE'S DRESSED IN sweatpants and a fuchsia sweater, and her red hair is in two braids. She goes straight for the kettle and fills it with water. Her morning is everyone else's evening. She starts her day selling beauty products just as everyone else is ending theirs.

Outside it's getting dark, and there's another #FearTheVillains gathering.

"How was school?" She's been asleep, so she doesn't know it lasted all of an hour for me today. I've been home since ten this morning.

"The usual."

She raises an eyebrow. "Really? On the first day back?"

"Well, the Watch was there, which was weird, but at least they kept the reporters out. Other than that, yeah, pretty standard."

"Was Lucas Attenborough there?"

"Yeah. He was lurking around." I think of his strange behavior, how he wasn't with his friends, how differently he was dressed; and it almost seemed like he was concerned about me or something. "We didn't talk."

"I wouldn't think so. You're going to stay away from him, right?"

"Yeah. He's not going to do anything to me with everyone watching."

She nods and grabs a couple of pieces of bread. "Anyone else?"

"I saw Morgie. She seems good. She misses Ursula, but it looks like she's got friends and everything, so I think she's okay."

"Huh," she says. "Well, great. I'll call her mother this week, but I can't leave the building yet. Reporters are still calling and I don't want any of them swooping on me. They haven't been bothering you, have they?"

"Only on the phone, and I ignore them. I think they've moved on, G. I'm sure they're still hovering around Ursula's apartment, but they're not going to sit outside here in the rain for nothing. Pretty sure they know we're not going to be of any use."

"You're probably right." Gia shoves her bread in the toaster and turns it on. She likes her toast basically burned. "But I just don't know if I can manage my temper yet. It reminds me of when . . . Well, you know . . . We couldn't escape them for months."

Yes, I do know. I was little when my family was murdered, but I remember the flashing lights trying to get in and out of the apartment, and Gia screaming at all of them. She wound up on the evening news as the victim's "unstable sister," and we got a visit from Child Protective Services.

"Take your time, G," I say. "There's no rush."

"So that was it? School was fine and everything went smoothly?"

"Mmm," I say noncommittally, hoping it's enough to get her to change topics.

I'm going to have to talk to Gia about getting expelled from school soon enough, but not five seconds after she wakes up and not when I haven't had the chance to figure out how I really feel about it. She's just as liable to shrug it off as she is to go completely ballistic and demand to speak to the superintendent and raise holy hell. I'm delighted when she turns back to the stove and hovers over the kettle.

"I ordered a couple of space heaters. Should be delivered today. If this weather keeps up, we're going to have to find a more permanent solution," she says. "I had to pull out my clothes from when I had that job in Midcity all those years ago. Glad I kept that box around or I'd be freezing to death. I suppose we'll need to look into installing heat eventually."

I'm so used to our apartment building I sometimes don't see all the ways it's crumbling, but crumbling it is. The appliances are old, the furniture rickety, and it could definitely use a coat of paint. I was going to finish high school and get a job on the squad, move through the ranks and make my way up the ladder in Monarch. I know I would have been able to do it, to help Gia with the money. Now I'll have to find another way.

"Turn on the TV," she orders. "I want to watch the news. Have to keep an eye."

I finger the necklace James gave me last year. Hearts on black leather. I remember how excited he was when he presented it to me. I also remember how he watched as I pulled it from its sack and let it fall between us, dangling in the light, like it was made of diamonds and not silver.

"There could never be enough hearts," he had said, closing the clasp around my neck.

"You're beyond cheesy," I said then. "They should lock you up in cheeseball prison."

"Ay," he chided, "can we steer clear of the prison jokes? A little too close to home."

For a second, I thought he was actually upset that I was insensitive enough to mention prison when his dad had been there since before we met, but then he started laughing. "You're right, I'm a huge cheeseball when it comes to you. Man's got to have a soft spot."

I punched his stomach lightly. "Yeah, and that isn't it."

He pulled me in for a long kiss then, one so good I forgot I was supposed to be at the station in Monarch and almost got myself fired my second week on the squad. Maybe if I'd blown off the internship, we wouldn't be here right now. I would have been paying closer attention to what was going on with him. I wouldn't have been so self-involved.

I couldn't always wear the necklace back then. The draping silver seemed wrong for someone trying to be taken seriously interning with the cops, but I put it on the night of the battle and I haven't taken it off since. The weight of it reminds me of the way I was once loved.

I bring up the note app on my phone while Gia chatters away in the kitchen.

Antidote? I type. I'm not a scientist, so that's a tall order. The first thing I need to do is find my friends. I need to talk to every single person who might be able to help me find them before the Watch does. I type:

> *Jack Saint*
> *Dally Star*
> *Bella Loyola*

Jack Saint is Mally's dad. He and Mally are so close I think she might let him know where she is, or at least that she's okay. He might have a line on something. It's worth a shot. Dally owns Wonderland, the bar where we all hung out. There was a tunnel that went from the lab where Kyle Attenborough was holding James, Mally, and Ursula right into Wonderland's storage room. It seems like Dally would have to know something about that, although it's hard for me to believe he would do anything nefarious. He's one of my favorite people, and I have good radar for scum.

Do you? the voice asks. *You didn't sniff out that chief, did you? Maybe not as tuned in as you thought.*

Last but not least, there's Bella, my partner from the squad who was fired immediately after the battle. I assume she hates me. I didn't listen to her warnings, and sure enough we got in huge trouble, everything went to hell, and she lost her job, which was the center of her universe, definitely the most important thing in her life. She had built her entire identity on it. My throat tightens at the thought. I feel awful.

Aunt Gia is fussing in the kitchen. She pulls a mug from the cabinet. The kettle whistle blows, sending a sharp note into the kitchen, making us both jump; then she pours water into her teapot and sniffs the rising steam with pleasure just as the toaster dings.

A cry comes from outside, a roar from a crowd of pro-testors. "DOWN WITH CAPTAIN HOOK! DOWN WITH CAPTAIN HOOK! DOWN WITH CAPTAIN HOOK!"

"Shut the hell up!" I yell out the window, but it doesn't even make a dent in the racket.

I used to think it was the luckiest thing that we lived next to Miracle Lake, even if it is deadly. It's beautiful, crystalline, the kind of place people are drawn to, especially with the floating lanterns all around it. But now because the battle happened near Miracle, it's the natural location for related protests.

"Oh, Mary, for the love of Fantasia, why do you insist on looking? Leave that outside where it belongs," Gia says, testing her tea for temperature.

"I can't help it," I say.

The crowd is gathered around an effigy of James with a dagger through his heart, face leering, left arm an oozing, bloody stump. Even in this crude form, I can see the outline of his face, his sharp jawline. It's a lifeless mockery, but it resembles him enough that

I can remember him holding me, his breath as he bent down to say something in my ear, that insular space in our relationship that belonged only to the two of us. The crowd attacks him, pulls him apart, piles him in pieces, and sets him on fire. They roar as he burns.

"Caleb Rothco!" Gia says, pointing to the TV. "It's time for the roundup!"

I slam the window shut, grab the remote, and turn up the volume. Monarch police arrested Caleb the day of the battle. At first, they charged him with the murders of Ursula and Mally, but as soon as it became apparent that they were alive, the police slapped him with a new set of charges. Caleb Rothco, aka the Mad Hatter, infamous criminal, is staring outward at the screen, his face impossible to read.

Just last week when Bella and I were still on this case, we found information on Ursula's burner phone about some argument she was having with him. We went to his tattoo shop in the Scar to investigate and found that Caleb gave Ursula a tattoo of a giant squid on her thigh just before she disappeared. Between that and the way he was acting, we thought he might be connected to her disappearance. He insisted the day he gave her the tattoo was the only time he met her, but I never quite believed him.

Little did I know then he was the self-proclaimed Mad Hatter, and had been leaving chopped-up body parts all over Monarch. As Bella and I circled in on Kyle and Lucas Attenborough, Chief Ito claimed Caleb had murdered Ursula and Maleficent, which would have neatly solved their disappearances, and no one would have looked for them again. That was all blown when they both turned up alive and had an epic battle on this block.

Caleb has admitted to killing a few Legacy traitors, and now, because it turns out he was trying to overthrow the local government, the DA has brought additional charges of sedition against him. That's treason, and if he's convicted, it'll be off with his head.

As it turns out, carving people up is frowned upon, but not as much as political extremism.

On TV, a journalist stands in front of the court building, facing outward, a crowd of reporters behind her, each turned to cameras from their news stations, each dressed in coats and scarves, pastel leather gloves warming their hands.

"Kristy, what can you tell us about the wild world of the mysterious Mad Hatter?" The news anchor in the studio is Narrows and is in the usual suit jacket with slicked-back hair and unnaturally orange skin.

"Bob, it's certainly been a day to remember here at the Monarch courthouse. Caleb Rothco, aka the Mad Hatter, a monster best known for leaving body parts around Monarch in gift boxes and terrorizing its locals, is now making a name for himself with his flair for the dramatic, and he didn't disappoint. He stood on the table, did illusion tricks for the DA, and impressed with his outlandish outfit. Admirers flocked to court, trying to pass him notes and get close to him. Word on the street is that he's . . . Dare we say it? Highly attractive! Today, the so-called Mad Hatter left spectators wondering whether he's a folk hero or a madman. If you weren't glued to your televisions, phones, and computers like so many Monarch citizens today, here's the highlight reel."

The camera switches now. Caleb is on the stand in a burgundy velvet suit with a black, sequined tie and top hat. He has gloves on his hands and tattoos peeking out wherever there's skin showing and he's gotten rid of his goatee. His cheekbones seem even more defined, and his eyes are darkened with shadows.

Oh, he is something, isn't he? She says.

"Shhh," I snap.

"I didn't say a word," Gia murmurs.

The lawyer asks him a question, and Caleb sits up tall, towering over the prosecutor, who looks weak and overblown next to Caleb's stringy certainty. I guess from a certain angle he *is* sort of highly attractive, but there's something shifty and unstable about him, as though his atoms and particles aren't quite as put together as those of everyone around him and are continually rearranging themselves.

Caleb clasps both his hands and leans forward. "What gives you the right to question me? That's what we need to consider, philosophically."

For a second, it looks like the DA is going to object, but then he scans the grand jury, probably trying to determine whether this outburst will work in the prosecution's favor. Apparently he decides it will, and he gives the courtroom a look that says, *Oh, here we go*, and smiles as though he's willing to play along.

"This is a court of law, Mr. Rothco," the DA says. "That is the nature of these proceedings. I ask you questions and you answer them, isn't that the way it goes?"

Caleb stares at the DA, his face a neutral mask; then he lets his lips part into a grin. A glint of a gold tooth sparkles from the lights, and cameras click and flash.

"You think you've caught me," he says slowly. He takes in the jurors one by one and connects with the camera, before finally settling on the DA again. "You haven't caught me. I'm beyond you and beyond your cages. I'm beyond your crooked laws, your leaders, and good and evil. I'm beyond anything you could ever understand. And you think you can keep me locked up, you think you can put me in handcuffs and lead me away and I'll stay there? I've only stuck around this long because I want you to understand exactly how powerless you really are." He lets out a shrill laugh. "You're like a mouse, eating a piece of cheese with no idea your back is about to be snapped."

The DA straightens his jacket, blanching. "So you're saying you're going to disappear?"

Caleb leans back, still taking the room and everyone in it into his possession. "What I'm saying is that everything that's happening is my will, even the fact that I'm here right now."

The DA tries to laugh. His equilibrium is lost, and he sputters, "Well, that's incredible, Mr. Rothco, because here you are, shackles on your ankles, answering for your dastardly actions. I don't think you're beyond anything at all. I think you're just a small, ineffectual criminal, and as soon as you're put away for good, this entire city will go about its life and you will be long forgotten."

"Objection," Caleb's lawyer says from across the room. "Judge, I'm not going to bother clarifying why this is completely inappropriate."

"Sustained. Mr. Rothco is innocent until proven guilty," the judge says. "And we'll keep our personal judgments and opinions out of these proceedings, counselor."

A wave of titters passes through the court, but Caleb stares straight at the DA. I clutch at my shoulders. From here, Caleb's eyes look black and like they don't have irises, like he isn't human.

"I apologize, Your Honor," the DA says.

"I know where you live." Caleb taps a temple. "And I never forget a face."

The DA freezes. "Are you threatening me, Mr. Rothco?"

"I'm informing you so you're not surprised when we meet again."

A wave of commentary rises through the court. The DA looks to the judge, but she remains impassive and just as riveted as everyone else.

"You've decided I'm a criminal for wanting to defend my people, the people of the Scar," Caleb says. "Everything about your government is corrupt." His words stick and slide all at once.

"Everything about what you're trying to impose is irrelevant to me. I didn't do half the things you're accusing me of, but I did do the other half, and if that lands me in the chair, then so be it. I didn't let this arraignment happen so I could answer your meaningless questions about where I was on such and such a day and what I was doing." Caleb looks directly into the camera, and I swear I feel like he's staring at me. "I was fighting for my people. I am always fighting for my people." He raises his wrists, shows the courtroom his Seed mark. "Legacy Loyalty. Loyalty is royalty. Legacy for life. We will rise, mark my words. But you . . ." He sneers, then looks directly into the camera again. "You're just a poor unfortunate soul."

Wait. *Poor unfortunate souls.* There it is again. Ursula's pet phrase. I may not know where my friends are, but the rumors are coming from somewhere and they are founded on something. I add Caleb Rothco to my list of people to talk to. I don't know how to achieve that though.

He's in solitary confinement at the Monarch PD, Mary. Just a train ride away.

She has a point. I do know how everything works there. I know exactly how to get into those cages.

I think back to the night of the battle, to the feel of the hatchet in my hand, purpose, adventure.

You liked the feel of the blade in your hand. You liked the feeling of cutting into flesh.

And then I'm there. Friday night. James is lying in the dirty street, in the hot and sweaty dark, the sound of helicopters circling above us as Monarch does its best to respond to the unprecedented threat of a dragon flying overhead and a sea monster the size of a skyscraper stomping around. But the monsters they're looking for are no longer in the form they're hunting them in. They're human size and standing in the street with me. We're all watching James die from being shot with a poisoned dart right in the hand he had raised to protect us. His fingers are turning black at the tips. The sound of the helicopters and the sirens in the distance slow and blur together, then come apart, each whine, each blade cutting through the thick air one *chuff* at a time. Everything has slowed, each second drawn apart as I try to think, think what to do next.

Maleficent, who's standing over James, says something about not being able to magically sever a limb, and I know that it's up to me to save him. I have passed the neighborhood hardware store thousands of times, know that the mannequin in the window has on a yellow vest, a plaid shirt, green boots, and that it holds a small hatchet with a red handle in its plastic hand.

I can't hear what Mally and Urs are saying. I can only see James splayed across the pavement, eyes closed. I know if someone doesn't take that hand, he'll wind up dead with poison in his heart.

I tell them I'll do what needs to be done, and I run, smash the glass with a swift, hard kick, and yank the ax from the mannequin. I charge back over to James, stand above him, and that's when I hear Her voice.

Yes, She urges. *Cut it off.*

And then I do. I raise the ax above my head and bring it down hard. It slices through James's flesh, through bone, through muscle and ligament, and then his hand falls to the sidewalk. I pull my belt from its loops and wrap it as tightly around his forearm as I can before Mally cauterizes it and a bandage appears.

I fall to my knees over James, lay a hand on his cheek, trying to get control of my breathing, which is coming fast and short.

Yes, Mary, She whispers. *Excellent. Off with his hand.*

I jump when there's a loud knock at the door. The highlight reel has finished, and Gia turns off the TV.

"Who's here?" I say.

"What do you mean? It's Monday night!" a loud voice calls.

"Oh pixie dust, the Naturalists," I say.

"Well." Gia looks offended. "You could be a little more gracious. They love you."

Gia bounds for the door. The Naturalist ladies bobble in like geese, all talking at once, Ginny and Cindy right up front.

"Can you believe it?" Ginny says. "The Watch is outside."

"A complete and total invasion of privacy," Cindy says.

"Now, now, now," Evelyn says. "We can't bring negative energy in here, ladies. Everyone take a moment to center."

The fidgeting sounds of jackets being removed stops, and they all close their eyes. Mattie holds on to the opal necklace at her throat. The room settles with new warmth. Evelyn is sweet; Mattie particular and incisive; Ginny is maternal and generous; and Cindy is a natural and fierce leader. All together they bring peace and wisdom, but they're also a lot.

Cindy sighs and raises her arms before letting them fall to her sides. Everyone starts talking again. Kisses are given on the sides of cheeks, jackets are hung on the coat tree by the door, and hugs are administered like comforting medicine.

"Gia, I know you baked something, so where is it?" Cindy asks.

And just like that, they're all fetching plates. Gia sets a new pot of water to boil on the stove and gets the cupcakes out of the fridge, and Mattie hands them out.

"The Watch was outside?" Gia says, glancing at me.

"They were, they were," Mattie says.

"They have to do something. Five children gone," Evelyn says, chewing thoughtfully. "You can hardly blame them for wanting to protect the Scar in some way. Maybe the Watch has our best interests at heart."

"Oh, don't be ridiculous," Mattie says, marching into the kitchen for the kettle. "This is about control."

"It's about Mary Elizabeth," Cindy says, and a hush falls over the room.

"You're one of the only links they've got to James and the rest of them. Of course they're going to keep an eye on you and on James's and Ursula's families. Of course we're going to get the treatment, too. Otherwise all they can do is run around the city like chickens with no heads, showing up when another Legacy teen has disappeared, and what good does that do? So they're watching you and keeping tabs on all of us just in case."

"I heard," Mattie says, pouring tea into cups, "that James Bartholomew's father made an announcement from prison." She lowers her voice to a whisper. "He says he's proud of his son, and whatever he's planning, he supports him. Says James has always been smart and has always been pro-Scar. Legacy Loyalty and all that." She tuts.

"Five of our babies are gone," Evelyn says. "No one knows where. It's worrisome, worrisome. Irresponsible to encourage it. He should be ashamed of himself, but then again he's a Bartholomew—"

She stops midsentence, noticing perhaps for the first time that I've gone very quiet and that Gia is gripping the handle of her teacup so hard it shakes. I don't like it when people lump James in with the rest of his family. He's not like them at all. He's good. Or at least, he was.

"She didn't mean it," Cindy says, giving my shoulder a squeeze.

"I don't know why I go anywhere with you," Ginny says to Evelyn.

"Well," Mattie says, trying to smile cheerfully. "Any new tricks up your sleeve, Mary, or is it still just the occasional levitation?"

All eyes were already on me, but now I feel them drilling with laser focus.

What am I going to say? *No, no, ladies, there's been no more levitation. It was just the once. Now it's only the odd voice in my head.*

"I think I'll take your advice after all," I say to Gia.

"What advice?" Gia says nervously. "What did I say?" She puts her cup down.

"You said I should go spend some time with friends."

"When did I say that?"

"When we were talking before."

"I don't remember that. And the Watch and the newspeople—"

"Screw the Watch," I say. "Let them follow me if they're going to."

"Can you at least tell me where you're going so I don't worry?"

"Sure." I look around at all these women with their colorful scarves and oil-scented wrists. I love them and am grateful that no matter how everything changes, some things stay the same, but I can't stand to be here for another minute with the pressure building in my chest. So I lie. "I'm going to Wonderland," I say.

FOUR

WHEN I GET OFF THE TRAIN IN MIDCITY, I CHANGE into a skirt and button-down shirt in the subway bathroom. I pull on stockings and the Thumper ankle boots the young and the rich around here wear in the snow and rain. I complete the look with a wool coat and top it off with a pastel blue scarf. I bought the outfit last year when I first got my internship in Midcity, lucking out when I found the boots on sale, but I never could bring myself to wear any of it. I'd assumed I would need to dress like I was from the Narrows to fit in, but it turned out one of the reasons I'd gotten the internship was that I was Legacy and they wanted me to be just that when I was working. When I wear the items, it feels like I'm in someone else's clothes, and I want to rip them off. I remove my usual dark eye makeup and put on a neutral palette, a light peach lipstick, and brown mascara instead of my black. I give myself a final once-over before tying my hair into a bun at the base of my neck. I've never seen anyone from the Narrows with hair left wild and free like mine. I look transformed.

I can almost believe I was raised rich and without magic.

I exit the restroom, stick my nose in the air and my shoulders back, and march forward. If Urs could see me now, I would never hear the end of it. And James? Instant breakup.

Midcity is kind of beautiful in its own consumeristic way. It's early November, with a more biting cold than in the Scar. The skyscrapers dominate everything, rising up in thick gray stalks, yellow windows climbing their sides. It's the time of year when people begin to turn inward and go shop for gifts and . . . I don't know . . . artisanal cheeses. The gritty glitz and glitter of the Scar is gone, replaced by trench coats and briefcases, sharp-angled packages, suits and ties, and sensible shoes. Shops line the streets, and for the first time I can remember, people I pass smile and nod at me. So this is what it feels like not to be a pariah when walking around in this neighborhood.

I think through my plan, which is of course really not a plan at all. I'm relying on the fantasy that the makeup and clothes will be enough of a change that I'll fly under the radar. I'm also relying on the heavy turnover at the office, that the newbies who have to work the front desk will have no idea who I am and won't make any connection between me and the hazy photos from the night of the battle. That's three things that have to go my way. I happen to know that Detectives Colman and Mahoney won't be here, and the chief and her assistant, Mona, are likely to be sequestered in the chief's office if they're still around this late.

I steel myself against my nerves and march up the stairs to the building that houses police headquarters.

"Help you?" the security guard says. He doesn't seem to register any alarm or recognition.

"Heading upstairs. I'm afraid I need to report something to the police."

He nods. "Got another hour before they close up shop."

"I know, I know. Train was delayed. Silly me." I lean over as casually as possible. "The truth is, there were afternoon cocktails. It can be so hard to find the right way to make an exit."

"I'll bet," he says, like he's tasting something bitter. "Party all the time in the Narrows, right?" He types something into his computer. "All right, show me your ID and sign in."

I pull my wallet from my back pocket and reach for the fake ID I had made just for instances like this, where I'd rather my real name didn't get involved. "Petunia Clarke" is eighteen years old from the Narrows, with an address at a boutique hotel in case anyone goes looking for her.

I smile as sweetly as possible as he enters my information. I've never been able to feign innocence, so I'm careful not to go too far. Something about me reads suspicious when I try. He hands me back my ID, then ushers me through the security system, hands me a stick-on badge, and points to the elevator.

"Good luck," he says.

Once I'm out of sight, I press the button for the third floor. As soon as the light flickers yellow, the nerves set in, and I feel like adrenaline is spewing everywhere. It's not just what I'm heading into, it's that I've somehow genuinely managed to avoid thinking about what happened the last time I was here. I try to remember that I'm on camera, to keep my head at an angle that will hide my face, and to be as still as possible so I look normal. As the elevator whirs upward, I remember the last time I was here. It's only been a few days, but it feels like a lifetime.

The day after the battle, after I'd been at the hospital and then the station all night, the police, no longer my colleagues, interviewed me, then escorted me into the main room to get my things from my desk. I was not the same as I'd been before. Cutting into James's flesh changed me, but it wasn't just that. There was a new electrical current in me from the shot Lucas had given me, and it felt like it was going to burn me up from the inside out. I'd begun to understand that what happened right after I got the shot was dissipating, that I'd had something like a reaction to a vaccine, and it had caused all sorts of side effects that had now calmed. But I knew something more permanent was happening inside me.

Yeah, She says. *It was me.*

Meanwhile, the station house was in chaos. All hands had been called to action, Kyle and Lucas Attenborough were both in custody, and Caleb Rothco was handcuffed to a chair in the center of the room. He'd nodded at me as I'd shuffled by, but I barely paid attention to him. I had too much to worry about to acknowledge his presence.

Gia had been stuffing a box with my things when the chief walked in. I didn't react at first; instead I'd watched her glide through the room with Mona trailing behind. Charlene Ito with her impeccable silk clothes and shining jewels, with her beautiful, regal face and her calculated, graceful movements.

She didn't even look at me. She didn't look at anyone.

As I watched her march through the station that night in such a commanding way, I couldn't help wondering how this was the same person I had watched pass an envelope to a shady guy with a dagger tattoo on the street two days before. At the time, I assumed it was a payoff to frame Caleb Rothco, since I'd seen the same guy in his shop when I went in, but it could have been anything. The fact remained that Charlene had lied about finding proof that Caleb killed Ursula and Mally, which was indisputable, since they were completely alive. She had fired me and then fired Bella, who didn't deserve to be fired at all, and then she didn't even have the decency to face me. It all left me feeling furious and personally betrayed.

So I smelled her, watched her stride, that smug line to her lips, and then I attacked.

I blew past Gia and ran for the chief with nothing in my head except the idea of hurting her, making her pay for what she'd done. I wanted to rip her face from her skull.

Even though I didn't scream or make any noise, I didn't get very far. Gia got a pretty good grip on me before I reached Chief Ito, and then a few of the cops who were milling around the coffee launched themselves between us. I screamed then, the frustration too much for me. I needed the feel of Charlene's flesh coming apart in my hands.

The chief had stood, unscathed, in the center of all those bodies. She didn't lose her poise for an instant, and the smugness only grew and spread over her features. She looked so cold and so obvious, I couldn't believe I had ever trusted her or that she had ever been a role model for me. She was plainly and completely . . . evil. I had been a fool.

Mona had eyed me fiercely as I'd fought against those holding me back.

"Don't move, chickadee," Detective Jones said in my ear.

Of course that sent me writhing, but he'd only gripped me tighter.

"You've got a lot of nerve," Mona began, pointing a finger at me. "After everything the chief has done for you. You completely disregarded her orders—"

"Stop." The soothing command dripped from the chief's lips. "Mary Elizabeth, stop this instant." There was no venom behind her words, no heat, but I went limp anyway. The chief had been my hero, and she still had an effect on me I couldn't quite put my finger on. It would take me another day to realize I still wanted to be wrong. I still wanted Chief Ito to be good.

"Come on," Detective Jones said. "Let's go."

"No," the chief said. "She's had a difficult night. No sleep. The incident with the ax. We have to remember she's just discovered her friends are pathological criminals. Who will it serve for her to be arrested? She's already been interviewed and cleared. She needs to go home." She looked around. "And we need to find the villains. Everyone, get to work." Her gaze fixed on me, and I found myself frozen in place. "Take care of yourself, Mary Elizabeth. I admire your tenacity and your passion, but do not come in here again. If you do, you're likely to find me in a less generous mood." And with that, she was gone, disappeared into her office.

As Gia had shuffled me out, my box of things between us, Caleb Rothco stared at me with a huge, toothy grin. He'd raised his hand in a greeting and then let his fingers fall one by one as though they were settling across the keys of a piano. His eyes followed every step I took toward the door, and just what had happened when I first met him, I'd felt them burning into my back long after we'd left the room.

"I hate her," I'd said to Gia as we left the building.

"I know," Gia had replied. "I hate her, too."

The elevator doors open onto the third floor, which houses the gym and the cafeteria, which are empty. One thing has gone right, and I need my luck to hold out a little longer. I scoot past the glass doors that lead into the station and push open the door to the locker room.

There's only one woman in here, and I don't recognize her. She's swaddled in a towel and leaning over the sink blow-drying her hair. I scoot in and crouch behind the lockers.

The cops lift weights and use the gym, but there's a popular aqua-aerobics class at this time every night, too, which means there will be uniforms I can grab. I check on the woman again, and she's still focused on her task.

Oh, please, if there's still any magic in me, let it help me now, because now is when I need it.

Don't worry, honey. I got this.

A calm washes over me, and I open the first locker. Nothing. I try the next one and the next. Just as I open the final locker in the row, the woman stops drying her hair and the place is suddenly too silent. Fortunately for me, I'm staring at a police uniform with an ID lanyard underneath. I move as fast as I can, pull off my clothes, and shove myself into the pants and button-down shirt. I pull the hat down on my head and tuck in the shirt as fast as I can, then get the ID around my neck. I grab the bag I brought with my Scar clothes and make straight for the door without looking back.

"Justine!" the woman at the sink calls. "Is that you?"

I tilt my face just a touch toward her and wave.

"Have a good night!" she calls. "See you bright and early! Overtime all around!"

I scurry down the hall imagining every terrible person I might run into, but none more terrifying than the chief herself. I'm impersonating an officer right now. That carries a hefty sentence. But it's more personal than that. Or rather, she would take it more personally if she knew what I was doing, and I have a feeling crossing the chief on a personal level would prove to be seriously problematic for my well-being.

Next I'm to walk into the jail, using my ID to gain access, and move as quickly as possible to Caleb Rothco's cell. They'll be shutting down visiting hours and doing checks as soon as it's time, so I want to get in and out.

I glide through the doors. I look at no one. I know most of the officers that work down here have little interest in visitors from upstairs. There are only a dozen holding cells here, and there's only one secluded enough to warrant placing someone as polarizing as the Mad Hatter in it. If they actually think putting him in a full-blown prison would get him killed, even with solitary confinement as an option, he must be in the cell in the back, which is why I'm going to need the special access key from the control room.

Everything is attitude, toots, She says. *No one dares question a queen. Act like one and you won't ever have to explain yourself to anyone.*

I use my pass to open the control room door, nod a good evening to the guy watching the monitors, and pull the key from its hook.

"Checking on Mr. Rothco on behalf of Chief Ito."

He waves at me, uninterested. "Give the Mad Chatter my regards." He chuckles. "Look out, that guy'll talk your ear all the way off."

"Will do."

Although I want to sprint to Caleb Rothco and get answers to my questions about my friends, I force myself to walk, one foot in front of the other until I get to the cell around the corner, secluded at the end of the hall. Its glass face reminds me of the hall of cages in Kyle Attenborough's building. I was in one not so long ago and could be in one again if I'm not careful. My chest tightens, and I focus hard.

I know exactly what this particular cell looks like, but it still takes me by surprise when I see Caleb, cross-legged on the floor in front of a table, calmly sipping a cup of tea. I've seen his face splattered across every TV screen, in every newspaper, dominating the landing page of every news organization, but now he's right in front of me, and it feels like it was way too easy to get to him.

And . . . he looks like he's been expecting me.

That's because this was meant to be, She says *It's fate.*

As I approach, he places his teacup in front of him and steeples his hands under his chin. I imagine him sawing up human bodies, putting them in boxes, and distributing them around town, all in the name of Legacy Loyalty.

Terrorist. Fiend.

He stares right at me, smiling. "That you, Mary Sue?" he says, still smiling. "Nice getup."

"It's Mary Elizabeth, actually."

He lets out a gentle laugh.

"Come on in," he says. "Let's chat." When I hesitate, he holds up his hands. "Look, Ma, no weapons."

I turn the key in the lock and scan the ID card so the door opens, and I pass through.

"Have a seat," he says, and motions to the patch of floor across from him.

"I'm okay standing," I say.

He nods. "I'm sorry I can't offer you tea this time. I've finished the pot."

Tea is a Scar tradition, and the last time I saw him we had a cup.

"It's okay. I didn't come for tea."

"So what did you come for, Mary?"

"Why aren't you surprised to see me?" I ask him.

"Everyone wants to see Caleb. Lots of visitors. All sorts. I had the mayor up here, the chief . . . all wanting to know what I know. But they still can't get in here." He taps his temple and stares at me like an ancient snapping turtle: languid movements, no hurry at all. His words are carefully enunciated, but his eyes crackle. "Why don't you ask me what you came to ask me?"

I hesitate. If he knows what I'm talking about, it means there's hope for me, that my friends didn't disappear into another dimension, that I might be able to see them again, to rest my head against James's chest, to laugh with Ursula until my stomach hurts, for life to be more than gloom and doom every second of every day. But if not, I'm not sure what I'll do next. "You said something during the arraignment today."

"I said lots of things. It was a good day for me, don't you think?"

"But you said one thing in particular."

"One thing?"

"Yes."

"It sparked something in you? Made you come all the way up here? Leave the Scar behind?" He lets his eyes flutter shut briefly. "I miss the smell on the street, of city and sweets, looking up into the sky and seeing the clouds shifting. I miss my people. These stooges in the Narrows have no idea what it means to live, to stand for something, to be the Seed for magic."

"No," I agree. "They don't." There's a larger conversation to be had about the people who live outside the Scar, but we can't have it now. One look at my phone tells me that aerobics class is going to be over any minute. I have to hurry up. "You said the people who don't understand the Legacy Loyalty movement within the Scar are poor unfortunate souls. Where did you hear that?"

"Maybe I made it up. Sounds good, doesn't it? Catchy?"

"The thing is, Ursula, the girl you tattooed . . ."

"The sea witch, the big bad villain—"

"Sure. I guess that's what they call her now, so—"

"Go on."

"Well, you know she was my best friend, that I came looking for her at your tattoo shop, that she disappeared a few weeks ago."

"She came back, though, didn't she? Back with a vengeance, one might say."

"She liked to talk about poor unfortunate souls. In fact, she said that phrase a lot, and she's the only person I've ever heard say those words."

The smile is returning now, sliding across the bottom half of his face, like the snake tattoo rippling from his collar. "I suppose I did pick it up from her, now that I'm thinking about it. She might have told me that Mary, Mary, Quite Contrary would know what it meant."

My heart constricts, and I try not to show my eagerness. "You've seen her? She had a message for me? Where is she?"

He doesn't move. "Oh, she's everywhere."

"Where exactly?"

He shrugs, smiling.

I growl. He's playing games. I'm not in the mood for games right now. There isn't time.

Caleb raises his eyebrows. "Temper, temper."

"Stop talking in circles. You're toying with me, and this is serious, life or death."

He considers me carefully. "Here's the thing. All I've ever wanted is to make the Scar a better place to live, to restore it to its former glory." He grits his teeth. "But I mostly want to get out from under the Narrows. So I'm going to do things they can't even imagine. And you. You made a choice to stay a prisoner when you could have had everything. You could have had magic and been with those people you supposedly love. You could have made a difference, but instead you decided to stay in chains. And now you're feeling remorseful about your choice. Not so sure anymore. You want to find them. For what? You think they don't know what's happening? They're *magic*. They can do things you can't even conceive. You rejected them, not the other way around. Remember that."

When James and Ursula asked me to join them, I surveyed the destruction all around me and chose to go another way, the way of the law, of regular life, a safer life, I guess. . . . And look where it got me: friendless, alone, and standing for nothing. But also, now I *know* that Caleb knows something more than he's saying.

"Seeing myself through your eyes, I guess I can't blame you for your low opinion," I say, and I mean it. Caleb may be locked up and he may even be dangerous, but he's not a coward like me. "But I just want to see them again."

"If you want to see them, you're going to have to find them all by yourself."

"Why? If you know something, why won't you tell me?"

He looks down at his fingernails, then back up at me. "That's not how the story goes, is it? You have to find the truth in yourself before you get what you want."

"What? What do you mean?"

"Uh-oh. I think you may have a problem." He cups his ear. "Listen."

A whooping noise is coming from another floor, a faint warning.

"Where'd you get that uniform, Mary Sue?" he nearly whispers.

"Pixie dust! I have to go." I scramble to my feet. They're going to come looking for me.

"Wait!" Caleb says. "I do have one little crumb for you."

I glare at him. I don't have time for this, but I can't walk away.

"You have magic you don't even understand," he says. "Ursula told me if you came looking, I should tell you. Look to the magic you have planted inside you and let it grow."

"What magic?" I press.

He shrugs. "Ho-hum. Another conversation for a different day."

I turn around. I'm not going to get any more out of him, and I have to get out of here. "Legacy Loyalty, Mary," he calls. "Never forget who you are."

And then I'm walking as fast as I can without drawing attention to myself. If I run, they will catch me. I don't look back.

Don't see me, I think. *Don't see me.*

People in uniform rush past me going the other way. I don't meet anyone's eyes but don't look down, either. I'm just starting to believe I actually have the power of invisibility when I hear a voice.

"Hey, newbie."

I look up, sure I'm about to be busted, but it's an officer I've never seen before. I'm not dead in the water yet. "Things are heating up in the Scar. Curfew violations. They called an 'all hands on deck.' Are you on duty?"

"No, sir. I'm heading home." I hesitate. "Is that what all the kerfuffle is about? The Scar?"

"Afraid so. So much civil unrest down there." He glances at my wrist, which is covered so he can't see whether I'm Legacy or not. "Interesting people in the Scar."

"Sure are."

"Which way you headed?"

"Home," I say. "Uptown."

"Okay, you get some sleep now. We're in for long hours and lots of pressure with the villains and whatnot. Make sure you practice self-care."

"Yes, sir."

When I push out into the cold night air, I get to the side of the building as fast as I can. I change into my Scar clothes and dump the other two outfits in the closest trash can. Back in my own boots and my black jeans and leather coat, I feel like I can breathe for the first time since I came out of the subway station.

And now I have something I didn't have when I walked in.

I know my friends are alive.

And they want me to find them.

FIVE

I WAKE UP THE NEXT MORNING TO THE SOUNDS of Gia shrieking at the TV. This has been her ritual ever since last Friday. Every morning, after her night of global "magical" cosmetic sales, she gets ready for bed, braids her hair, makes me a fresh pot of coffee and bedtime tea for herself, and she yells at the television until she's hoarse. There are myriad issues for her to address: riots, rallies, hourly commentaries on Ursula and Maleficent and James, demands for all citizens of the Scar to contact authorities if they have any information. She practically spits whenever Kyle Attenborough appears. Whatever's irritating her is my new alarm clock. Except today there's a new urgency to her routine, enough so I leap out of bed and run into the living room.

"Fairy godmother!" she says, like she's had the wind knocked out of her. "Shattered wand!"

"What is it, G?" I'm still trying to bring the room into focus and also stay standing, since I got up way too fast and am on the verge of fainting.

Gia is dressed for bed, horn-rimmed glasses on, skin glistening with serums and creams. She spares me a glance and then goes right back to watching. "It's all over the news!"

"What?"

Gia points.

The reporter on TV is speaking from outside the Monarch Midcity courthouse building, surrounded by other reporters doing the same, but that's how it's been every day recently, so it's nothing new. She's not what has my attention. Under her in bright, bold letters flashes:

CALEB ROTHCO HAS ESCAPED / NO ONE IS SAFE / STAY HOME / LOCK YOUR DOORS / FEAR THE VILLAINS

I sink into a chair at the dining table and keep my face as blank as possible.

"Can you believe that?" Gia says. "He's just gone! Poof!"

"Did he—" My voice wavers, and I pinch my wrist to steady myself. "Did he Vanish?"

"No!" Gia is practically squirming. "Some woman let him out of his cell. They have footage. I'm sure they'll show it again."

The thumping in my chest picks up speed. I must have left the door to his cell open. I don't even remember what I did with the key card. I was so panicked about the alarm going off I don't remember much at all besides changing next to the building. I fill my lungs and empty them out, and I try to think.

The newscaster talks and talks, and just when I think she'll never shut up, the screen cuts to grainy surveillance footage from the night before. A woman in leather is walking down the corridor past Caleb Rothco's cell. Her face isn't visible, but her hair is long and curled and red, and the way she walks—no, slinks—sends chills running up and down my arms.

"Who the hell is that?" I say.

"They're calling her the Red Queen," Gia says. "See that crown on her jacket?"

Sure enough, the back of her red leather coat is embossed with gold. Everything about her terrifies me: the way she clings to the side of the hall like some kind of spider, instead of walking normally; the way her jacket almost serves as a corset, giving her an unusually small waist; the way her hands seem to be reaching for something, and how Caleb rises to meet her, hugs her, and follows her out of the cell like she's the Pied Piper.

"Wait, wait, wait, what did she just say?" I ask, blinking hard.

"What?"

"About the time? The reporter. What did she say?"

Gia looks up from her tea with brows furrowed. "That the time stamp shows she was in his cell just before seven p.m.? Why?"

That aqua-aerobics class finished at seven. The siren went off at seven. That Red Queen person wasn't in the cell. *I* was. But I wasn't dressed like that, I was in a uniform, and Caleb definitely didn't follow me like he did her. He was still sitting on his floor when I left.

"Are they sure?"

"It says it right in the corner of the footage." Gia rewinds the news and pauses it as the Mad Hatter and the Red Queen are leaving the cage. "Six fifty-seven. Why?"

"Nothing. No reason. That just seems like odd timing for an escape. It's not midnight or something."

Except there was that siren causing total chaos. Everyone was running to get to the Scar because of the fights that had broken out after the Watch and the cops tried to enforce the curfew. There was probably no one watching the jail or the key or anything else until hours later, and with the siren already going, it looks like he escaped without much of a fuss at all.

But none of that explains how she was there at the same time as me.

"Can you turn it back to the live feed?" I say, barely able to get the words out.

Gia scrunches her nose at me but complies without complaint.

The reporter is back on. "City officials consider this woman extremely dangerous. Anyone with information about the Red Queen should contact the Watch or dial 911 immediately. She is being added to the list of most wanted villains, along with the Mad Hatter, Maleficent, Captain Hook, and Ursula. Citizens are reminded to fear the villains and to use that hashtag whenever they are sharing information on social media."

The screen flashes red, the reporter disappears, and the screen is blank. There's no more news, no reel spitting out the latest, no pundits commenting on the dire situation in the Scar. I'm about to tell Gia to turn the TV off and on again to see if that will fix it, when big, bold letters flash across the TV. HEADS WILL ROLL, it says. Then there's a crackle and the news feed is back on, a roundtable discussion underway.

Heads will roll?

My throat has dried out, and I can't swallow. "Did you see that?" I croak, already knowing the answer.

"See what?" Gia says, and my heart sinks.

I am not well.

"Nothing." My knees weaken, and I thump onto the couch. "Can you turn it off?"

"Oh, first she wants it on, then she wants it off."

"Gia," I beg.

Gia's face softens into concern. "Okay, sure, sure, honey." She yawns. "You all right? Have fun at Wonderland?"

For a second, I don't know what she's talking about, and then I remember I told her I went to Wonderland last night. "Yes. Yeah, it was great to see Dally."

"Good. Good old Dally Star," she says, not saying the rest. That he's the only person I really care about who's left besides her. "I guess you'd better get ready for school, then, eh? Forget about all this for a while."

"Yes! Right! Definitely!"

Wow, how many lies am I going to tell this woman before breakfast?

"Okay, I'm going to bed. You have a great day, and we'll have a longer conversation tonight." She stands and stretches. "It's getting stranger and stranger out there, Mary. I can't wait for everything to get back to normal."

"What is normal?" I don't mean to ask such a philosophical question when she's trying to go to sleep, but I for sure have no idea what normal is anymore. Maybe I never did. The Scar and everything and everyone in it are the furthest thing from normal.

"Well," she says, giving me a small smile. "Normal such as it is, then." She comes over to me and strokes a cheek. "Don't you disappear on me. I don't know what I would do."

She heads for the bedroom, and I'm left standing in the living room, the image of the Red Queen a little too familiar to be ignored. I can't deny that my reality is wobbling. I'm seeing things, time isn't functioning right, and I'm hearing voices. That Wrong Magic is making me feel upside down, and I don't know if I can believe my own eyes anymore.

I need help, even if it's from someone who might be really, really hostile.

I pull out my phone and tap out a text to Bella and hit send before I can change my mind. I need someone, and Bella's the only person I can think of who will have an objective perspective on this situation. For now, I can only think of the next right thing to do.

And that's to go see Bella Loyola.

SIX

THE WHOLE SUBWAY RIDE TO BELLA'S, I HAVE
first-date nerves. I should be at school doing school things, not
being shuttled across town wondering if I'm ever going to feel
right again. I struggle to keep my knee from jumping, and when a
nice elderly lady tries to strike up a conversation with me about the
Mad Hatter, I shut her down immediately.

I'm trying to think about what I'm going to say to Bella that's
going to keep her from knocking me sideways when I get to her
house. She told me to come over, but there's no way we're going to
avoid at least a conversation about the fact that I didn't listen to any
of her advice before the Battle of Miracle Lake and she wound up
getting fired. I'm basically responsible for every bad thing that has
ever happened to Isabella Loyola, who was doing just dandy before
she met Mary Elizabeth Heart.

Okay, maybe that's an exaggeration. I have Dr. Tink in my ear
telling me how I can't be responsible for anyone else's happiness and
how we all have to find wholeness inside ourselves. Still, I'm pretty
sure I messed things up for Bella in a major way.

She probably won't understand that I lost my dream, too. I had
a vision of myself as a woman. I knew who I would be. I would fight

for the Scar from the inside. My clothes would cling pleasingly to my form, still me but mature in some way I couldn't grasp from my little-girl vantage point. My face would age with deep wisdom about the ways of the world, and no one, no one, would mess with me. James and I would marry. We would have our children, and he would turn his questionable street dealings toward business, maybe run a bodega or a small restaurant. We would show the Scar what life could be. We might not have magic, but we would be proud Legacy, restoring dignity to our neighborhood and our family reputations. I would rise through the ranks and wear shoes that clacked on marble floors when the occasion called for it. I would be me but better; me but all-the-way me, the full expression of my potential.

I watch it all evaporate right in front of me, get sucked out of the train car and disappear into the tunnel. That person will never exist now.

Lucky you, She says. *Sounds like a total bore.*

Maybe I should see it as a clean slate. I'm nothing and no one now, and anything is possible. I have no future and no plans for the first time in my life. Only one thing. One goal. One drive. Get to James. Everything after that is up for discussion.

I walk the couple of blocks from the train station to Bella's house. If there is such a thing as a swanky neighborhood in the Scar, this is it. Set away from the industrial and commercial parts, the houses are bigger and stand-alone, instead of brownstones and apartment complexes stuffed with Legacy. This is where the Narrows have demolished old houses and rebuilt their fancy new mansions. Flowers line the streets, and the pedestrians look like they belong uptown. Bella's house is dirty white, huge, with impressive columns and a scratched-up sign that reads HOUSE OF FANTASIA in faded letters painted on the outside of the building. This was once the greatest wish-making house in all of the Scar. People came here when they had something they really wanted, and it was said that if you braved its doors, you were sure to emerge with your destiny in hand. My parents met here, which led to me, then my sister, Mira, then to their death. Some destiny. So maybe that accounts for the extra weight I feel as I approach the door and rap the curlicue rococo knocker.

I'm ready for Bella's mother or aunt to answer, maybe angrily, or for Bella's reproachful gaze, for her judgmental appraisal of my outfit, for various sniffles and splutters, and maybe even an altercation, but I am not at all prepared for what greets me when the giant door swings open.

Bella is a mess. Not the usual adorable level of dishabille that's her trademark, a somewhat lopsided ponytail, a casual slouch to her pants, her flawlessly natural makeup. This is something completely different.

Great ghost!

Bella Loyola is in sweatpants.

A T-shirt hangs off one shoulder, and I'm pretty sure I'm looking at some sort of gravy stain.

And . . .

I want to hug her so badly. She's water for a dying plant, ketchup to french fries, tail to a mermaid.

"Mary Elizabeth?" She squints and blinks rapidly, like the light is hurting her eyes.

"Yes, hi. I texted you? You told me to come?"

"I know you texted me," she says, and I exhale. "I responded, remember? I'm not in*sane.*"

No, but *I* might be.

She puts a hand on a hip and makes an exasperated noise, then takes a look to the left of her stoop and another to the right, grabs my forearm, and drags me into the house, slamming the door behind me.

"Were you followed?"

"I'm always sort of being followed," I say. "But no, I don't think so. At least, I didn't notice anyone."

I was all ready to have to give a statement of apology before I could tell her why I wanted to talk to her and what was going on, but now all that slips away as she drags me into the foyer.

"No one at all?"

"No."

"You can never be too careful these days. Caution, caution, caution. That's the ticket. The Watch and all that." She squeezes me, and I smell something musty, like she hasn't showered in a few days. Bella usually smells like a summer flower, fresh and simple and lovely. "I'm so glad you got in touch," she goes on. "You're the only person I know who's both Legacy and a detective."

"I'm not a detective—"

"Blah, blah, neither am I anymore. Irrelevant."

Our voices echo. Half a sandwich lies on a plate on the dining table that looks three days old. Fantasia and Stella, Bella's mother and aunt, usually have a stream of delicious treats flowing, festive music playing in the background, and frequent laughter, but there's none of that now, and the house feels empty and somehow austere in spite of the warm, inviting decor.

"Where's your mom? Your aunt?"

"Oh, they went to some convention for a week," she says absentmindedly. "Something about learning to live magically without actual magic. They eat and get massaged, basically." She keeps looking in the direction of the ballroom like she can't keep her focus on me.

"Listen," I begin. "I want to say I'm sorry for—"

"I don't want your apology." She finally settles her gaze on me, and the compassion I find in it is unsettling. "You've lost so much."

"I'm fine," I say. "I'm practically a walking suit of armor."

"Mm-hmm," Bella says doubtfully, "no feelings whatsoever, right?"

I smirk, but the joke hurts. I have too many feelings. Always too many. And Bella knows it.

"Listen, Mary, you're the only person who will ever understand what's going on," she says gently. "You're the only one who was there, the only one who lost more than me during the battle." She takes my hands in hers. "I've been wondering and worrying and feeling so alone, like there was no way out of this awfulness and I would be buried under the weight of it all. But then your text came through, and it was like the fairy godmothers had all gathered together to give me a sign."

I pull my hands away and open my mouth in mock surprise. "Did you say *sign*? Do you have a fever?" Bella is the most logical person I know. It would take something earth-shattering for her to believe in signs. I palm her forehead like I'm going to check her temperature, and she bats me away.

"Oh, for magic's sake," she says, but there's a slight smile playing at her lips.

"I think you need a therapist immediately."

"All right, all right," she says, "that's enough."

If she weren't Legacy herself, Bella would probably be one of those people who denies magic ever even existed and thinks the whole thing is a hoax.

She smiles a little sadly. "Things have changed for me."

"Because I got you fired."

"No, no, no, no!" She waves me off, and I notice her nails are stubby and cracked. "Let's just say I've progressed as a person very, very rapidly. As for the rest of it? Bygones. Seriously. Don't give it another thought. What else were you going to do? You had to find your friends and your boyfriend. But in the end you did the right thing, even though you were tempted. You didn't go with them even though you wanted to. You were ethical, which isn't easy, and I'm sorry I wasn't there for you, that I was too busy feeling sorry for myself to reach out the last few days."

"No. I don't deserve that—"

Bella takes my hand and gazes at me earnestly. I brace myself. This is when she's going to dig even deeper, to talk to me about James, about the chief. This is when I'm going to have to keep my emotions in check and not allow myself to fall apart like I want to. But instead of having a heart-to-heart, she yanks me through the door to the living room.

"Hey! What are you doing?"

"We don't have any time to waste. I told you it's a sign that you texted me when you did. Have you seen what's going on out there? I mean, have you seen the news? The fights last night? I heard the windows at the Tea Party got smashed out."

This stops me. The Tea Party is an iconic part of the Scar, owned by James's godmother, Della, yet another person I haven't been to see since the battle. She must be wrecked.

"You didn't know," Bella says.

"No. I didn't."

"I'm sorry, Mary. I really am."

"Yeah, me too."

She squeezes me.

"I want to show you something," she says, changing gears. "Can I?"

"I'll do pretty much anything if you'll stop manhandling me."

"Shh," she says, and covers my eyes with her hands. "Just let it happen."

I want to whack her, but I laugh instead.

After another solid yank, I feel the air open around us as she leads me into the ballroom, where Legacy used to hide from their magical duties and relax. It has high ceilings and complicated columns with crown molding that looks like wedding cake, and drapes made of Parisian pink satin. I know where I am because the air smells vaguely of bubbles and fairy dust, some kind of magical residue. This is a place where so much magic once happened it hasn't quite left, and there are traces of it everywhere.

Bella lifts her hands so I can see.

"Great ghost," I whisper.

I'm looking at the most elaborate, detailed mind map I have ever seen. There are pictures of people lining the entire wall, newspaper articles, printed-out emails, and each one is connected with a piece of string so the whole thing looks like a spiderweb. It extends all the way to the ceiling, which is about fifteen feet high. This one puts the scribbles we made in the conference room at the station to shame. There's a rolling ladder nearby, the kind usually found in libraries. Bella clambers up to adjust a photograph a few feet up.

When she gets down, she places a hand on each of her hips. "This is my masterpiece." She indicates the map. "Monarch is a bastion of corruption, just like I thought, and all I need are a few more *teeny-tiny* things to prove it."

"When you say *teeny-tiny*—"

"I'll get them," she snaps. "I'll find a way. The truth always comes out. It's a universal fact. They've done the dirty deeds, and they're going to be brought to justice."

"Bella," I say carefully, "I don't think that's actually true. People do bad things all the time and don't get caught. Look how many cold cases there are, murders people never have to answer for. And politicians have been taking advantage of their positions forever. It's how the world works."

Bella eyes me severely.

"So what are your missing pieces?" I ask.

"One, I need to find proof of collusion." She points at the string that links the chief to Kyle and Lucas Attenborough. "Kyle and Lucas were experimenting on Legacy kids, right? You know as well as I do that there's no way Kyle just waltzed down to the Scar, discovered the greatest secret there is, bought a building, and built a tunnel connecting his lab to Wonderland without anyone knowing. How did he find the source of magic? How was he granted whatever permits he needed to build his lab? Who built him that tunnel?"

"I don't know," I say.

"My money's on the chief." She glances at me.

"She never comes down here. Barely even acknowledges she's Legacy."

"Exactly. It's perfect. But you're right, you're right, I can't prove it. What we do know is she's crooked. We saw it ourselves. She paid off the guy with the tattoo. She framed Caleb. She did everything she could to keep us off that case when we actually started to crack it. So that makes her a suspect in my book." She takes a breath. "And then there's Dally. I'm sorry, but I just have a feeling he's involved."

"The tunnel is hard to overlook," I say. Dally is the friendliest, most artistic person around. He's so busy planning events and running the bar, I can't imagine him having any interest in all this. But I have to admit he does look like he must have some part in it.

"Then there's Jack Saint," she goes on.

"Mally's dad? But he would never allow Mally to be experimented on."

"Right. I think something maybe went wrong, but it would make sense if he's involved, because he's the richest guy in the Scar."

"Right. And he's friends with the chief."

"Exactly."

I let my eyes drift over the wall, up and down over the pictures, the maps of the Scar and all of Monarch; I look at the mug shot–type pics of Mally, James, and Ursula, and home in on the one of the chief, the Mad Hatter, Kyle, Lucas, and Jack Saint. Then there are the newspaper articles that have come out in the last few days, all about the villains, the Watch, the fights in the Scar, the rallies, and emails that look like they might be between Bella and the police department, and inquiries for paperwork from the hall of records. I land, finally, on a picture of me and follow the cords from me to every single one of the people in question. I am connected to all of them. In some ways, it looks like I'm at the center of this whole thing.

"There's more," she says.

"Hit me."

"Well, the other day I was lying there with, you know, several cartons of ice cream or whatever—"

"What flavors?"

"Irrelevant."

"Flavors," I insist.

"If you must know, I enjoy a vanilla."

"Shocking."

"And strawberry."

I give her a look.

"The point *is*, while I was eating said ice cream, I realized that this whole thing is one giant scam."

"This whole thing?"

"The villains thing, the Watch, the spin on Caleb, *definitely* the spin on Kyle Attenborough. It's all a bunch of rotten, stinky garbage. So I started doing research, research I never would have had time for if I were on a case. Dots started to connect, and it stopped being such a dizzy mess." Once again, she beams at the wall and flails her arms in its direction. "This is what I figured out."

Bella taps her toes, looking from me to the wall and back again.

"You're literally stressing me out so much right now," I say.

"Okay, look!" She drags the ladder over and scrabbles to the top. "Here's the chief." She indicates the row of pictures beneath. "Here are all the police and detectives we *know* are corrupt. Then over here." She scoots herself over and makes dramatic invisible circles. "These are the people who are *probably* corrupt or involved in some way."

I recognize Mayor Triton, Kyle and Lucas Attenborough, the Mad Hatter, and several of Chief Ito's underlings, plus the housing commissioner and the zoning-committee chair. There are a bunch I don't know. Then I see threads from the chief to my friends.

"They're not connected!" My friends have never had enough pull or been important enough a day in their lives to know anyone in governmental power until Lucas lured them to his dad.

"They're not *not* connected, either," Bella says. "The chief is behind it all, everything. I know it."

Bella's obsession with the chief might be sending her over the edge. I'm not sure she can see clearly.

"In what world do my friends have anything to do with the chief?" I ask.

"Ah!" She climbs down the ladder excitedly. "Bear with me here. The chief gave the money to the guy with the dagger tattoo." She points to a drawing of a silhouette with a giant question mark in the center. "And *he* was in the Mad Hatter's tattoo shop the day we went in. And *Ursula* got her tattoo from him, and now he's escaped from jail, and you can't possibly tell me that's a coincidence, too, because I won't believe it. There's an order to things, a clear and profound order. And you cannot convince me that this is not part of a larger pattern. Just because I don't have every single piece yet—"

"Or any evidence—"

"A detail that can be remedied. I mean, this is not right! The police aren't even doing anything! And don't you dare tell me this doesn't have anything to do with the Mad Hatter and why he was in jail for all these things he says he didn't do."

For a second, I don't know what to say.

"What?" she says. "I know that look. What are you thinking?"

"I talked to him last night."

"Who?"

I take a deep breath. "Caleb Rothco. The Mad Hatter. Right before that Red Queen person set him free."

She has me by both shoulders in a flash. "And? What did he tell you?"

"A lot of nothing. He talks in circles."

Bella releases me and flops onto a nearby chair with her thinking face on. A strange silence descends over the room, and then she looks up at me. "These people are going to tear the Scar to shreds and sell it for parts," she says. "I don't know why and I don't know how, but if we don't stop them, everything that's happened so far is going to feel like an afternoon in the park."

I watch her a moment, trying to absorb everything she's said, before my eyes flicker back to that wall. All those people. All those pieces. So many lies.

"Okay, this is the last of it," Bella says. "I've spent a lot of time thinking about this. Pretty much every second since they threw me out of the station, and you know what I think?"

"Tell me."

"I think the reason magic disappeared in the first place was because the corporate moguls in the Narrows were starting to find ways to mass market it, and that is not what it's for. So I think magic decided to leave until the residents of the Scar recognized that and started behaving responsibly. But did those in power leave it alone? No, they did not. They messed around until they found the source."

"And what was that?"

"I don't know. But I will. It's coming from somewhere, and Kyle Attenborough figured out what that somewhere was. I know that much. And I'll tell you something else. Magic didn't take the assault sitting down. It may have been discovered, but it decided that if they wouldn't leave it alone, it was going to come back in a way they had never imagined." She points to the pictures of James, Mally, and Urs. "And that's where *they* come in. They aren't villains. They're delivering a message on behalf of magic itself that if residents of the Scar don't start handling their business, all hell is going to break loose."

I plop down on one of the lovely little cupcake poofs that pepper the room. I want to argue with her, but I can't. I think she's right. There's so much I can't share with Bella, not yet. One of those things is the night I was with James in the Ever Garden, when he first showed me he had magic. He must have already been in talks with Lucas Attenborough, visiting that lab without telling me what was going on. I'll bet he thought he had it all under control.

He produced a blue light in the palms of his hands that night. I knew it wasn't just a light, and it wasn't that it seemed to come out of nowhere or that he made it from nothing that made it special, although that was a spectacle.

It danced, leaped, *communicated*. It brought us closer together, bound us, and when it went into my chest, I felt it filling me up with warmth and intensity, but also something else.

Intelligence. It seemed to have a mind.

"How did you get to this?" I ask.

Bella purses her lips and looks upward. "It's what makes logical sense. If you think of magic as a sort of *person*, like a fairy or a mermaid or something, it must have a personality, and if it has a personality, it must have moods. Every being has them, after all. Think about how it's always been good and then it got taken advantage of. Actually"—she smirks at me—"I've started thinking of magic as more of a *she*, and she has been getting treated like a doormat for years now. What happens when we get walked all over?"

"We get pissed off," I murmur.

"We get ticked off," she agrees. "Really, really ticked off, and that's what's running through James and Mally and Ursula right now. That's what's running through you."

I wish I could go back now and instead of being so stupidly trustworthy when he showed me that light, demand that James tell me what the hell was going on. I wonder if the magic he gave me that night is made up of the same thing as the magic Lucas shot into me. I levitated with the Naturalists *before* Lucas. I saw the girl in the mirror *before* he gave me that shot.

You're getting warmer, She says.

"What are you thinking, Mary?" Bella says. "Am I way off base?"

"Not necessarily," I say, pacing in front of the mind map. "But I think you're right. There is a source."

What I don't say is that if we can find the source, we might also be able to find an antidote, and if we can find that, I may be able to make the so-called villains come home, go back to normal, and make everything return to the way it was. That, and maybe if I can find out where the magic is coming from and who stands to gain from it, I can finally find out where my friends are.

It's a shot, which is a whole lot better than nothing.

Our eyes meet, and for a second, I think she might cry. She

doesn't want to be alone any more than I do. All her defenses and nervousness fade away. She sniffles a little. "It hasn't been easy. I was so mad when the chief fired me." She reddens. "It just makes me so upset, especially knowing she's terrible."

"The chief is crooked, but none of this is proof that she's directly involved in the experimentation or the Wrong Magic. Even seeing a guy take an envelope from her isn't proof all by itself. We don't know there was money in the envelope. We don't know anything at all. And we're never going to get past all this theorizing"—I wave my hand around—"unless we get real concrete evidence. So let's get out of our heads and into the real world and get to detecting."

"We?" She bats her eyelashes in such an adorable fashion I want to hug her again. She smiles huge. "Detecting?"

"Yeah, *we*. Bella, it's time to leave the house."

She throws her shoulders back. "Don't you have school?"

"Don't ask."

"I'm sorry," she says.

"Well, on the plus side, my schedule is wide open, so this is perfect timing."

"Oh bread-and-butterflies, Mary, this is wonderful!" She sweeps me into a huge hug and squeezes me so tightly I can hardly breathe. She leans back and looks at me. "There's just one more thing."

"Uh-oh. Spit it out."

"Stay right there!" Bella calls, then runs up the stairs and disappears.

I don't know what she's up to, but I seize the opportunity to take some deep breaths. A couple of minutes later, she takes the stairs back down two by two.

"My phone!" She's already typing manically.

"What are you doing?"

She bites at her bottom lip as her glasses slide down her nose. "The first thing we have to do is find the tattoo guy who took the envelope from the chief. We need to find out what was in it and why she gave it to him. We can't ask Caleb because he's gone, but I know just the person. She's brilliant and a whiz at this sort of thing. She'll find him in no time." She taps the screen. "Here she is. Jasmine Bizhan!" She hands me the phone triumphantly. I prickle. What we're planning to do is already risky, and adding another person feels like an unnecessary risk. I don't care if she's a whiz.

"I don't know. A stranger? What we're doing isn't exactly on the up-and-up, and I don't think anyone would appreciate us snooping around. Don't you think we'd be better off keeping it just the two of us?"

"She works at the paper. She's in obituaries or something awful and is looking for anything at all to give her the story that's going to break her out of that beat. She has a press pass and access to town hall. What do you think is going to happen if we show our faces in Midcity right now asking questions?"

It would not be good.

"And you trust her?" I ask.

"She needs a big break as much as we do. We can build trust on that. Let's go find her."

"Okay," I say, a little reluctantly. "Let's do it."

"Yes!" she says. "The gang is back together! The partnership is on!"

"Slow your roll," I tell her, but I'm grinning.

"I will not!" She types something into her phone, then looks up at me with shining eyes. The phone almost immediately beeps. "Well, this is just wonderful. She can meet with us tomorrow!"

"No."

"Yes."

"Yes?"

"Yes, tomorrow. Come on! I'll walk you to the station!"

"Absolutely not. I'm not going anywhere with you."

"You're right. It might look suspicious if we were spotted. The Watch and everything." She squints at me. "Wait. No. Why?"

I try my best to keep a straight face. "Because you need to shower. Like, right now." I point to the stairs. "I'll meet you here tomorrow morning."

"Tomorrow first thing?"

"First thing. I promise."

SEVEN

I MEAN TO GO HOME. IT'S JUST ABOUT THE TIME I would be getting out of class and Gia should be sleeping anyway, but after the first stop on the subway, a woman gets on and sits across from me. She looks normal enough, with a Seed mark, wearing sunglasses, a bright orange sweater, and some red corduroy pants, and carrying a shopping bag. But I feel like she's watching me, and I don't like it, so at the next stop, I get off and get back on in a different car.

Another minute goes by and I tell myself I was being silly, but then I look up and the same woman is watching me through the double doors in the other car, holding on to the bar when there are open seats all around her. She has no reason to be standing, and she is definitely staring at me from behind her sunglasses, swaying robotically as the train moves along the tracks.

When we get to the Miracle Lake stop, I don't move. If she's from the Watch, she must already know where I live, and if she's a member of the press, it's probably the same, but that doesn't mean I want to make it easy for her. Desire Avenue is next, so I go past my own stop, then when we arrive, I let the doors open, the people get off and the others pile on, and when the announcement comes to clear the door, I shoot out of my seat and through the double doors. Sure enough, as the train moves on, I see her speaking urgently into a wristwatch.

I run.

I jet up the stairs, past the ads for the opera, the theater, the comedian doing jokes about how great it was back when there was magic. I blast past the invitations to the Merrypetal Church for Magic Anonymous meetings and past the scores of posters with James, Mally, Ursula, the Mad Hatter, and now a new blank outline that reads THE RED QUEEN. I run up into the cold air and let the raindrops pelt me. I don't look behind me. My heart pumps blood through my body, thumping hard, and I run and run and run. I know.

And then I'm there, shaking and out of breath.

James's house sits right on the corner of Desire and Hope. It's always struck me as an odd name for the intersection, considering it's become the worst neighborhood in the Scar.

I'm instantly queasy. I always avoided coming here, even when James was around. The house is such a boy zone, each room inside with its own bunk bed, the Lost Boys scattered everywhere. But more than that, as proud as I ever was of James and who he had become, I always felt I shouldn't be here, that deals were happening, and that stepping into this place was equal to picking up a rock that had been undisturbed for so long it had formed an entire society of critters underneath. The boys ate, slept, played, and worked together in a pack. I never felt like I belonged here, and since James has been gone, it's like there's been a force field around the house, repelling me. I've spent hours on the couch playing video games with the boys or upstairs snuggled up to James, but this is most definitely not my territory.

All James's mechanical equipment is out, as though he was midproject when he left. His car, *Sea Devil*, sits majestically in the driveway. Several other cars are in various stages of undress, bits and pieces scattered alongside them, and for just a second as I approach the porch, I think I see James's silhouette, long and lanky, hidden in shadows on the ratty porch sofa. My heart leaps, but then I realize it isn't James at all.

The moody-looking figure on the porch leans forward and rests his elbows on his knees. He watches me closely as I near the stairs, his jaw set in a near underbite, bleached hair grown since the last time I saw him, dark circles under his eyes. The dog at his side growls.

"Barnacle," I say, and James's dog slaps his tail and whines, but he stays where he is.

"Yo ho ho and a hot cup of tea," Smee says softly. "I thought, I thought you'd never come."

The sound of screaming echoes out from the house next door, and I tense.

"Not to worry," he says. "Just a friendly domestic dispute. They'll go at each other all night and be fine by morning."

"There isn't any such thing as a friendly domestic dispute," I say.

"You may be right. I don't know what you want me to do about it. Things are tough all over."

"Yeah," I say. "Can I come up?"

He places a hand on his chest. "Mary, you hurt me. Of course. James's house is your house. You know that."

"Do I?"

Smee lets out a breath that's something like a laugh but not quite. Tattoos peek out from under his T-shirt, and I notice a new one that reads LEGACY LOYALTY. It wraps around his left arm in a band.

"Sure," Smee says. "I've been waiting for you to show up. Thought maybe you forgot about us."

"No." I want him to understand, but suddenly no explanation seems adequate for anything I've done. "I didn't want . . . I thought you might be mad at me."

"For ditching the captain? For not showing up for us? Why would that make me mad?"

"Can we go inside?" I don't want to be on the street. "Talk?"

"You know you're welcome in for a bite of food, but not if you want to talk. Those little wizard hats from the Watch have the whole place bugged to high hell." He looks past me, to the empty street. "You hear that?" he calls. "I know you're out there." He gives the air the finger. "Can't catch me, baby." He makes a clicking noise, and Barnacle clambers to his feet. "Let's go."

Behind Smee I can see the TV flashing and three of the boys, Wibbles, Damian Salt, and Starkey, eating fast food out of yellow wrappers, slapping at one another and laughing. It's good to know they're still here.

Smee gets Barnacle leashed and signals to me to follow him.

"You're going to leave your tools out?"

"Who's going to steal them? No one, that's who."

I kneel down and rub Barnacle's back, his sleek gray Weimaraner fur. He must miss James. Barnacle lays his head in my lap. I give him a couple more pets before Smee and I start down the block.

"Do you know where he is?" I ask.

I don't need a preamble to what I'm going to say. Much as Smee and I have had our problems, we've always had love for James at our center, holding us together, and that means something now.

Smee arches an eyebrow. "Do you even have to ask?"

"Then why are you still here? Why aren't you with him?"

"I could ask you the same, couldn't I? Only our answers would be very different." Smee takes a few steps. "It would be such a nice evening for a canoe ride on Miracle Lake," he says.

"You can't canoe on Miracle. No one can. The water's deadly."

"Mmm, is it?"

"Why is everyone talking in riddles? Is it some new trend I'm not up on?"

"Guess so," he says, then stops to let Barnacle relieve himself on a tree. He puts one hand in his pocket and crooks his head to the side. "That's what happens when you don't check in. You're not in the loop."

"That's not fair."

"Yeah, it is. It's exactly fair." A black car slithers down the street. Smee follows it with his eyes as it passes, raises his hand in a greeting. "Good evening, buttheads."

The Watch.

Barnacle's done, and we move on down the road.

"Can you take me to him?" I ask.

"I don't know what you're talking about." If the Watch is anywhere near us, they can listen in on our conversation, and Smee has shut it down.

"Okay," I say. "But if you do see him or hear from him, can you tell him I'm looking for him? Can you tell him I just need to talk to him? That I'm trying to find a way?"

"I haven't seen him. Can't help. Sorry." As he says it, he nods to me, checking up and down the empty street. He gives me a thumbs-up.

"How are the boys?" I say.

"The three that are left are doing fine. Got ourselves a skeleton crew."

I stop and look at him, wonder if I'm imagining a new energy in him, something sparkly and more feral than before. "Skeleton crew?"

"Yeah." He grins. "Didn't you hear? Murphy, Skylight, and Mullins all disappeared this morning."

"What?"

"Yeah," he says, with mock drama. "Craziest thing. We were having our pancakes, and poof. Just like that. Gone." He slaps my back, then slips something into my hand. I look down to find a set of keys held together by a silver snake pendant, then back up at him. "Some of us had to stick around and take care of Della, you know. You hear what happened to the Tea Party? We had to tie up some loose ends with all that." He shows me his fist and flexes. "People don't have any manners these days. Have to be taught." Smee leans in close and whispers in my ear, "The *Sea Devil*'s yours. James told me to give it to you when you came. Said to tell you you'll always be his girl. We take care of our own." He steps away and makes a clicking sound. Barnacle stands at attention, and then with another click we're moving back to the house. "Storm's coming. Let's make sure we're riding the waves and not drowning in them."

We've reached the house now.

"Want to come in?" he says in his full voice. "The boys would love to see you. It's just about teatime, and you know how they feel about that."

I smile. I don't know if it's because Della owns the Tea Party and James practically raised all of them, but teatime is a do around here.

"I'd love some tea." It was nice to see Bella, but this is different. This is family.

"Knucklehead," Smee says, and puts his arm around my neck. "You came just in time."

I'm just about to ask if he means because it's four o'clock, when the doors swing open and Damian Salt rushes me and picks me up in a huge hug. "I thought that was you, but then I thought, nah, she wouldn't come here, she's got better things to do than hang out with us, but *then* I thought, she loves us, of course she's come to see us! And here you are!"

Smee smiles, nudges me, and says, "You've been missed," then passes me by with Barnacle trailing behind, panting and searching for a treat.

Damien is only fifteen, but he's well over six feet tall and spends most of his time lifting weights, so he's got a bulky chest. He also has an awkward mustache situation happening.

Damien swings me around in a circle before putting me back down, then sticks his hands in his pockets. "You coming in?"

"'Course I'm coming in. I wouldn't not come in."

"Wibbles! Starkey!" he calls into the house. "Mary's here! Set another place for tea!"

"Mary?" Starkey says. He's smaller than the other boys and was always James's favorite. Actually, he's everyone's favorite, abandoned when his parents were killed in the Fall and raised by James since. Poor kid is only thirteen. "Come inside and see what I made!"

The living room has been festooned with ropes and pulleys that hang all around the TV and sofa and coffee table. Wibbles is on the couch half-asleep and raises one hand in a greeting when I walk in.

"What's all this?" I ask.

"Our boy's been busy," Smee calls from behind the doors that separate the kitchen from the living room. "You ready?"

"Yes! Let's do it!" Starkey leads me over to the couch and sits me down. "Stay right here and don't move a muscle."

"Okay," I say uncertainly. You never know what might come at you in this household. Starkey undoes a knot on one side of the room and the rope system begins to unfurl. As it does, a tray of cups with cake, sugar, cream, and a steaming pot of tea comes swinging delicately toward me.

I grin. This is genius.

Even Wibbles sits up and rubs at his eyes.

The tray lands right in front of me.

"Perfect!" Starkey says.

Smee leans out of the kitchen. "Oh, you're going to make the Cap so happy when he sees you again. Just imagine the possibilities."

Starkey beams while I try to make sense of what Smee's talking about. I'm about to ask, when Starkey says, "Well, go on! You get the first cup. Guest of honor."

I recognize the lemon butter cake from the Tea Party and the full savory scent of the tea itself. Della must be keeping an eye on the boys, bringing them food, or they'd be in much worse shape. I take a slice of the cake and pour myself some tea with plenty of cream and sugar. When I've taken my serving, Starkey pulls on the rope until the tray is in front of Wibbles, who takes his cup, and so on until everyone has some.

"So you're going to see James?" I ask unceremoniously. I take a sip and look around. No one will meet my eyes.

"You know what? I think I'll have a crumpet instead." Damien Salt stands and Starkey dashes for the ropes again, but Damien stops him. "No, no, I'll get it myself."

"I already told you we can't talk inside," Smee says.

"Understood," I say. "But I just want him to know one thing, and then I won't mention it again. I want him to know I love him and that I was wrong."

"Wrong about what?" Smee asks, leaning over one knee, heavily lidded eyes searching me.

"I should never have let them leave without me. Tell him that, okay? Tell him I said that."

It feels so good to watch TV and hang out with the boys that I stay until it's way too late. I text Gia and tell her where I am and that I'm going to spend the night here. She responds with a heart emoji and a text that says, *We need to talk.*

I have that to look forward to, whatever *that* is.

The boys have moved from video games to chess and are harassing each other when I mount the stairs to James's room. I used to love coming here, walking up this block, watching him move around inside the house, oblivious to my presence. James always has to keep moving. He likes to dust his shelves, shine his boots, to organize his books. He loves to read, especially about war and strategy.

His desk is perfectly clean, everything at right angles. His closet is sparse and organized, and his leather jacket hangs on the post of his headboard. I immediately go to it, put it on, and feel myself enveloped in him. How many times did he drape it over my shoulders? How many times did I rest and find my confidence in his love for me?

I let my head settle on his pillow as the rain starts up outside. When I close my eyes, everything immediately fades to black.

I wake to the sound of a ticking clock.

Tick, tick, tick, tick.

It echoes through the house so loudly it shakes the bed.

I press myself against the headboard and squeeze my eyes shut, waiting for Smee or one of the boys to run in the room and explain what's happening, but no one comes and the ticking stops as suddenly as it started.

When I reach for the lamp on the bedside table, the room stays black. I feel my way along the wall to the light switch, but it's not working. The electricity must be off in the whole house. I can tell by the profound silence. I get my phone and turn on the flashlight, wish I had my knife, my Taser, my pepper spray . . . anything to protect myself. I edge out into the hallway, hugging the wall, and it's completely empty. There's not so much as the squeaking of a floorboard. Nothing but the sound of my own breath.

And then the ticking starts up again. *Tick, tick, tick, tick.* I shine my flashlight from corner to corner, and there's no sign of anything anywhere. I follow the ticking down the steps, slowly, picking up its cadence. *Tick, tick, tick, tick.* I know where it's coming from as the sound fades before me.

James's study, the one room in the house he didn't like anyone to go in but him.

Sure enough, when I get to the bottom of the stairs, I find a great X scratched into the middle of the door.

"Very subtle, James," I say. "X marks the spot, eh, Captain Hook?"

The scrape rips through the wood, all the way to the doorknob.

The ticking stops as suddenly as it came, and I think, *He could be in there. He could be behind that door, waiting for you. Happy or sad, angry or reproachful, you could be about to touch him in the flesh.*

He is not there.

The office smells like him, residual musk and hard work, grease from the mechanical tools, but almost everything he kept in here has been cleared out. He used to love to get dressed up in a nice button-down and come down here to work on all his financials, get the boys organized, make sure everything was running smoothly. It was one of the only times you'd find him shaved and clean and so focused on normal everyday things.

Now the shelves are empty except for a few lone items: a couple of pens, a picture of Desire Avenue, a #LegacyLoyalty poster. There's nowhere for him to be hiding, nothing for him to crouch under, and why would he anyway? Even the curtains Della made for the windows in here are gone, stripped away. It's dark but with the very beginnings of dawn showing through the window, a low-hanging moon hovering close.

A glow starts up at James's desk emanating from a dark green box lined with gold, dipped in a lilting blue light. I rush over to it and pick it up and recognize it right away. It once belonged to my grandfather.

As though answering a call, my Seed mark throbs on my wrist. I pull up my sleeve, and the mark leaps, as though trying to separate from my skin, it's so hungry for the light. As soon as I pick up the box, the light sinks into my palms, and I'm in nearly painful bliss as it shivers its way through me before it disappears.

The room suddenly flashes red. I blink, but it's red behind my eyes, too.

You made the wrong choice, She says. *You should have gone with him. He still loves you, and you abandoned him.*

"I made the wrong choice," I say, clutching the box in my hand. "You're right. I made the wrong choice. James!" I call. "I made the wrong choice."

There's no response, of course, but maybe he can hear me, wherever he is. I don't know what the rules are anymore. Maybe he's watching me through a crystal ball, or maybe he's learned how to distort all the laws of time and space. I flip open the lid to the box, already knowing what I'll find.

Inside is the pocket watch I gave to James so many years ago when we were first together and I wanted him to know that no matter what anyone said about him, no matter even what he thought of himself, to me he was worthy of everything. He was . . . He *is* my family. He deserved to have my grandfather's pocket watch, one of my only objects of value. It was never as valuable as him.

When I lift the watch, a note flutters to the ground and lands faceup. *Keep it for me. —J*

Keep it for me. The watch, the magic, his heart.

He still loves me.

He isn't going to leave me here forever.

But I want to go now.

"James!" I call, running from room to room. I would feel him if he were here. He's not.

And neither is anyone else.

Smee is gone, Wibbles is gone, Damien Salt is gone, and even Starkey is gone.

So I'm here alone. There's so much I don't know. But it's not like I'm totally powerless. I'm going to prove to James, to Ursula, and even to Mally that I deserve at least to see them, to have a conversation with them. I want them back, and maybe if I can fix things on this end, they'll feel safe enough to come to me. There are many things I can't control, like where they are and what they're doing right now and why all those kids are disappearing. None of that has anything to do with me.

But there's a lot I can do. I can meet up with Bella, help her figure out the source of magic, find a way to get to Kyle Attenborough and persuade him to make an antidote to the Wrong Magic. I can work every second of every hour to get to the bottom of this, and that's exactly what I'm going to do.

I have a pretty good idea of where to start.

EIGHT

JUST BEFORE THE FULL LIGHT OF MORNING, I gather myself, stuff the watch and the note into the pocket of James's leather jacket, and leave his house in the *Sea Devil* as fast as I can. I'm pretty sure when the Watch gets wind of the fact that the rest of the guys are gone, this place is going to be crawling with them. They're not going to find anything incriminating. The whole thing has been cleared out. Even Barnacle is gone.

The Scar looks more or less normal. Everyone is out doing their morning errands, kids are headed to school, elderly ladies sit in chairs outside their apartments gossiping, and stray cats and crows pepper stoops and corners. Maybe the fights the other night were the outburst the Scar needed to ease into this new reality.

When I pull up to Bella's house, she dashes out, hair up in a bouquet of curls, blue-framed glasses, light blue sweater, and high-waisted tan cords along with some oxblood loafers.

"Where did you get this thing?" she demands, nodding toward the car when she swoops in, bringing with her the scent of grapefruit. "And what are you wearing?"

I look down, reddening a little. "I spent the night at James's.

I thought I was being followed and didn't want to go home. I got some of his sweats and one of his T-shirts. Is that a problem for you?"

"No! No! Unless you feel like borrowing something from me. I have the most delightful little pin-tucked—"

"No, no! I'm fine. I'll go home later. We have so much to do and I can't *wait* to meet your wonderful friend. . . . What was it?"

Bella narrows her eyes. "Jasmine. And do I detect sarcasm right now, and this is not the time for your antics."

"I'm not going to be full of antics, I promise." My Seed mark thumps impatiently. "We have a common goal. It's a good-behavior guarantee."

She puts a hand on my elbow. I can't feel it through the thickness of the leather jacket. "Okay, fine, I trust you. But I want to say this out loud before we go any further: I want us to have an understanding."

"What understanding is that?"

"If you see one of the quote-unquote villains, you will not keep it from me. There's too much at stake for you to act like a . . . well . . . *you!*"

"I will tell you if I see any of them," I say. I have not lied to her. I did not see James. I only saw *of* James. But if I did see him, would I run to her and confess? I would not. I would lie to her face one thousand times. "I promise."

"Great. Good." She leans back, relieved. "As for the car . . ." She runs her hand up and down the leather dash and grins. "It's a hell of a ride."

"Bella! How naughty!"

"Oh, hush," she says, straightening her glasses. "Now. Let's take care of business." She arches an eyebrow at me. "Well, drive, will ya?"

I follow her instructions as she screeches at me, first to make a right and then a left after a few more blocks, and there we are, back in the warehouse district of the Scar, right near where Mally used to live with her father, a giant, and a very persnickety maid, and as we pass her building, a murder of crows circles overhead.

"Mally's place," I say.

"I remember. Absolutely charming," Bella returns dryly.

I slow down as we pass the front door, and my heart nearly stops. There, all along the wall, someone has graffitied the words ALL THE WAYS ARE MY WAYS in bright red paint. Off to the right of the words is a little stamp of a crown.

"Did you see that?"

"What?" Bella says. "You look like you've seen a ghost."

"There was graffiti with a crown...."

"Oh, right! Yes, that's supposedly the Red Queen. You didn't hear the news this morning?"

"No." I try not to show how relieved I am that I didn't imagine the graffiti.

"It turns out they're finding her tags all over the city. Buildings are being defaced everywhere. Always in red paint and always with a crown stamp to the side. The Red Queen is coming for us all!" She draws out the words and makes spooky fingers before shaking her head and sinking back against the seat.

My Seed mark begins throbbing again like a second, more agitated heartbeat.

"Apparently she's warning the Scar about whatever is coming next. She's in cahoots with the villains and is acting as their spokesperson. Mayhem is coming, bloodshed, a reckoning for us all. There's a whole squad trying to decode it all."

"What's she saying?" I ask.

"Oh, a bunch of really dramatic, cryptic wizard guano."

"Like?"

"You know . . . Heads will roll, off with their heads, this is but a taste of what's to come—stuff like that."

Those are some of the things I've been seeing, thinking I was mistaken. Maybe I'm not losing it after all and really am seeing those things. Maybe it's everyone else who's not seeing it.

"Either way," Bella says, "she has everyone riled up."

"Not you, though?"

"Well." Bella gives me a sideways glance. "The graffiti could be some kind of copycat or something."

"What about Caleb Rothco . . . the breakout?"

"There's nothing to indicate the same woman who broke him out of prison is the same person who's graffitiing the Scar. Anyway, they'll find out who she is soon enough. Or who they are."

My stomach flops uncomfortably. "What do you mean?"

"There could be a bunch of villain lovers who are working together. There are already all those fan clubs cropping up. People are sick. Whoever they are, they're not going to be able to escape for long. There are cameras all over the Scar. They'll be working on it now, looking back to see what the footage shows. I'd wager they'll either be picking up some disturbed, bored person, or they'll be rounding up a pack of hooligans with no connection to the villains whatsoever."

"Yeah, right," I say. "Just a matter of time."

"You okay?" Bella asks. "You've gone stark white."

I clear my throat, try to pull all the scrambling pieces of my mind into coherency. "I'm good. Just thinking."

"Stop thinking and pull over. We're here."

The beat-up hole in the wall is decorated with a tarnished sign that reads THE GENIE'S LAMP, but honestly I never would have seen it if she hadn't pointed it out. In fact I'm sure I've walked by it multiple times without ever noticing it.

"Jasmine works at the *Genie's Lamp*? You said she works for an important paper. The *Genie's Lamp* is a total rag."

"Give her a break. It's a long story."

"Bella, if I had a dog, I would use this newspaper to pick up its poops and I wouldn't bother reading the articles first."

"I know. That's because no one wants anything but gossip. No one expects to be given real information from a paper generated in the Scar. They've got the *Monarch City Herald* for that. Why do you think we were the only two people from the Scar other than the chief who were on the police force? I don't want to get into a whole thing right now, but Legacy need to educate themselves and stop wishing for the good old magical days. If we don't occupy positions of power, we're in big trouble in the long run."

I put up a hand. "The Legacy Loyalty movement has changed that. People are moving in that direction."

"Okay, fine," she says. "But don't judge a book by its cover. You have to give Jasmine a chance. She has big plans for this rag . . . I mean, paper. Like I said, she's on obits. But if she can just break a story, a real one, they might have the chance to turn the paper around and to get some quality readership. Trust me . . . she's good!" She tugs on my hand. "And besides, we need her credentials if we have any hope of finding out what's going on. Now come on, please. I'll buy you coffee!" she singsongs.

"Before," I say. "Coffee before. Jasmine after."

The offices of the *Genie's Lamp* are not swanky. They are the opposite of swanky, though even through the window from the outside it's obvious there's a level of comfort to the place. Brilliant blue pillows accent the window bench, and there's a samovar on an ornate table. Other than small touches, the place is shabby and run-down, covered in beat-up desks as phones ring and reporters dash around, calling out to each other. There are big screens on three of the walls, displaying the news, and a whiteboard pulled out into the center of the room, marked up with different colors.

Tuesday Ideas
"Mad Hatter and Kyle Attenborough: Affair?"
"Sources Say Things Heating Up Between Maleficent and
Captain Hook"
"Ursula on a Kidnapping Spree: No One Is Safe"
"The Red Queen Actually Vampire?"

"They're bottom-feeders. Look at that board. None of that is true." My face heats at the mention of James and Mally. Back on the night of the battle, I kept getting the sense that they were a team, that they had a special connection. She wouldn't have stopped me from coming with them, but she seemed fine leaving me behind. They're in a stressful situation together, and I'm here. Anything could be happening.

But then I remember the pocket watch he brought me, the magic he left for me. There's still hope for James and me. Especially if I can find an antidote to the Wrong Magic. Anyway, I'm pretty sure Mally only wants what gives her an advantage, and all the muscle and street smarts James brings into her high-fashion, privileged life have to work to her advantage.

"They're Legacy trying to make enough money to survive. Shame on you," Bella hisses as she searches the room, then perks right up and starts waving animatedly. "There she is. Come on!"

A head pops up from the back corner followed by a hand that waves us over in her direction. She's hidden behind a partition, so I don't see her whole face until we get all the way inside her cubicle. Jasmine has long, thick black hair with jeweled barrettes holding it perfectly in place, brown skin, and wears high-waisted jeans and a blue silk crop top. I quickly check her wrist, and sure enough she's Legacy. She's following the newest trend, rhinestone stickers over the top of the Seed heart, which is something I usually hate, but on her it seems tasteful and attractive. She gifts us a white-toothed, open smile.

I immediately begin scanning her cubicle, where she has pictures of all the Vanished lined up and pinned to her wall; the only ones missing are the boys who went this morning. There's also the requisite flyer with James and Ursula and Mally splashed across the front, some shots of the woman in the red leather jacket with Caleb Rothco, and a pile of papers on her desk that I would love to get my hands on.

She pulls Bella into a tight squeeze. "I'm so happy to see you, my friend." They kiss each other warmly on each cheek. "It's been too long."

"Since graduation day, right?"

"Yes, and then it was like life took over and *zip*, two years have gone by."

Bella glances at me. "We both got undergrads in journalism."

"But Little Miss Overachiever doubled in CJ," Jasmine adds.

"That's criminal justice," Bella explains.

"I know what it is," I snap.

"And you got your masters in political science, didn't you?" Bella says to Jasmine while giving me a quick kick to the shin.

I force a smile.

"Started it," Jasmine says. "Life got lifey. You know how it goes."

I hate it when people say that.

"Jasmine's parents own the paper," Bella explains.

"Then what are you doing—" I start.

"On obits? I ask myself that all the time. My dad has this thing about everyone working their way up." She lowers her voice. "It used to be a really good paper, you know? But after the Fall, so much changed so fast, and my dad needed to keep selling papers or he was going to have to fold." She resets and plants a fresh smile on her face. "And here I am telling you all these things when I haven't even properly introduced myself. I'm Jasmine." She pumps my hand up and down several times. "You're Mary Elizabeth Heart, wunderkind, first-ever Legacy to win the youth internship with the Monarch City police, first-ever female under eighteen to be on a murder squad task force, first female under eighteen to serve in an active investigation—"

"First to get sacked, too," I say. "But nice job doing your homework."

"Enough to know you were at the Battle of Miracle Lake," she says, holding my gaze, "and that the enemies you were fighting weren't just villains to you."

"Can you believe this weather?" Bella interjects. "Whoever thought there would be thunderstorms in the Scar?"

"I know," Jasmine says, allowing focus to be pulled from me. "Absolutely atrocious. And you. It's awful the way they fired you."

They shouldn't be allowed to get away it."

"Aw, thanks for saying that," Bella says. "Onward and upward!"

Jasmine seems like an okay person, but I've never forgotten the lesson Ursula taught me early on: People need to earn the right to your trust. You don't give it away for free or you make yourself cheap. Also, she's a journalist and one who hasn't been able to break a story yet.

"I'm so sorry about what happened to your friends," she says, turning back to me. "It's just awful. Kyle Attenborough should have gone to jail. Anyone who cannot see that he's only down here to buy up all the property so he can monetize everything the Scar has ever stood for is just walking around with blinders on. Speaking of . . ."

Jasmine lifts up the chaotic pile of papers. "That's why I'm trying to break this story," she goes on. "The cops, city planners, witnesses, Attenborough's employees—they all had the same tale to tell. I mean the people I could even get to talk to me. All toeing the line. Kyle Attenborough's story is that he saved everyone from trying to go after dangerous criminal kids. In his latest statement, he says he made a mistake, because he should have done psychological profiling before giving them the magic. He says that if they weren't already bad, this never would have happened."

I feel myself heating up.

Attenborough should hang for that, She says.

"He's saying Maleficent was known to have oppositional defiant disorder and emotional disturbance as a result of losing her mother in the Fall, that James has criminal tendencies, and Ursula is sociopathic. He's saying the problem was in *them,* not in his serum. Either way, he says he feels responsible to make it right." She snaps to, seeming to realize I might be. "Oh, I'm sorry. I'm being so insensitive. It's just all I think about."

"It's okay," I say wearily. "I missed twenty-four hours of news, and look what happened."

"It's not okay," she says, coming forward to take my hands in hers. "Everything is happening so fast and not fast enough. But none of this is okay. Even if everything Kyle says about them is true, they still deserve better than what they're getting."

Bella knows I don't like randos touching me, and she's eyeing us anxiously while pretending to peruse Jasmine's desk.

"Those were your friends. James Bartholomew had been your

boyfriend for years. They were actual people with real problems. Just because they were poor Legacy doesn't mean they had . . . *have* any less value than the rich kids from the Narrows. It's infuriating." Jasmine drops my hands and steps back. "I know now is probably not the time, but if you ever wanted to talk to me, I would tell your side of the story—"

"You mean the truth?"

"That's right. I would tell the truth if you'd let me."

"You sure you don't just want to know the sordid details about my relationship with James?"

"To give you a chance to humanize him . . ."

"And you don't want to know everything there is to know about the giant octopus girl?"

"Well, of course people are curious," Jasmine says.

"No," I say.

Bella's face has fallen, all her features taut, shoulders nearly to her ears.

"No," I repeat. "And if you ask me again, I'm going to leave."

Jasmine concedes with a downward glance. "Understandable. I probably wouldn't want to tell the story to a stranger, either." It seems like she's going to sit, but then she suddenly begins pacing. "The thing is . . . Well, the thing is that we can't just shut down. This is the time to fight. And I know this newspaper doesn't have the best reputation ever, but if I can break one story, get the attention on us over here just once, we can change things for the better. I have all these pieces." She indicates the various piles on her desk. "It doesn't have to be you, Mary, or your story. Maybe there's another angle, another way to make people pay attention. I realize you're in mourning, you must be utterly traumatized actually—"

"I'm fine," I say.

"I'm just saying I know this must be hard for you, all this having affected you so personally, the whole town on the hunt for blood and that blood belonging to your most beloved people, but the way you can make the most difference is by being part of the fight! Both of you know what happened. . . ."

"Sort of," I say.

"More or less," Bella says.

"More than me," Jasmine says.

Outside, sirens blare.

I check my phone. "You know what?" I say. "We actually have to get going. It was great to meet you, but—"

"You're Legacy," Jasmine says. "I am, too. It's not easy. Much as we like a good party, we're private people and don't trust easily. That's why the Narrows and Midcity have always controlled the media and why it's always been so skewed to their agenda. I'm not doing that here. If you two work with me, you have my word I won't release any information until we're ready." She sees my hesitation and seizes the opportunity. "My people are wish-granters, a long line, some of the best at teaching people the lessons they needed to learn. You don't think the Great Death hurt them? Thank the blue fairy my mother is a good seamstress, or we would have been out on the street." I think of Gia, how she was on her way to being so famous in the magical beauty industry, and now she has to pedal her wares every night and has no life. "My father started this paper with dreams of making the Scar aware of all the injustice, and it got away from him. I know he wants it to be a real paper again. I know we can make it better than it's ever been."

Bella says, "You don't have to sell me on it. I'm game. I think it's time we get the rat bastards."

Jasmine watches me, saying nothing, but I can practically see thoughts zooming through her mind.

That's when I catch sight of something under a stack of papers on the desk. "Can I?"

Jasmine nods.

MONARCH LAB CORPS. I grab the document.

"I know there's something here," Jasmine says, "but I don't know what it is. I've gone cross-eyed trying to figure it out."

Bella comes up behind me. "Great ghost!" she says.

I pick up the whole pile, hand her half, and start riffling through. "These are Kyle Attenborough's financial statements," Bella says. "They aren't public record. How did you . . . ?"

"I have my ways," Jasmine says, twinkling.

"And these are deeds, all properties being bought up by . . . Hang on." The blood rushes to my face. "Oh no." I look up. "Kyle Attenborough owns part of Wonderland?"

"Yes. Is that a big deal?" Jasmine says.

"Well, yeah! The owner, Dally, is Legacy all the way." I look at Bella and she nods slightly, indicating it's okay for me to share. "I thought he hated Kyle Attenborough."

"Follow the money," Bella says, still sifting through the pile. "Isn't that what Maleficent's dad said to do? And look at all this. Attenborough's been writing monthly checks to Chief Ito? For what?"

"I bet Attenborough bought into Wonderland so he could make that tunnel that went from the labs to the bar so they could do all their experimenting more easily."

"Dally probably took the money because Wonderland was about to sink. Maybe that's the money the chief was giving the guy with the dagger tattoo. Maybe she's part of this, too."

"They've been giving Wonderland a face-lift, haven't they? An infusion from Attenborough?" Jasmine says.

"So many possibilities," Bella says, tapping her chin with her index finger.

"Wait a second." I yank a piece of paper from Bella's pile.

"Hey!" she says.

My heart begins pounding wildly. "*Reflections?* What is this?"

"It's a deed," Jasmine begins. "Some small company Attenborough acquired last year."

"Any idea what it is?" Bella asks.

Jasmine shrugs. "Probably a front for something. Or maybe he's going to tear the building down and put up another Mega Mega Mart. Who knows?"

I know what it is.

Yes you do, She says.

The sticker on the back of the mirror at Wonderland—the one I went through, the one I saw that ghostly face in—said *Reflections*. I memorize the address on the deed and try to keep my face still. This is not something I want to have to decide by council. I want to go to Reflections on my own.

"So, what do you say?" Jasmine asks, delicately removing the deed from my hand and placing it behind her back. "Do you want to join forces?"

Bella seems to be waiting just as intently as Jasmine.

"Sure, why not?" I say.

Bella and Jasmine high-five so perkily I have to let out a very long sigh.

NINE

SEVERAL HOURS LATER, BELLA CHECKS HER phone. My stomach is rumbling, and I've had just about enough of sifting through boring documents. "Oh, fudge, that's Aunt Stella. They just came back from their getaway and are unhappy about the mind map taking over the living room. I have to go take it down. Aunt Stella says they're ready for a new start." She straightens her stack of papers and shoves them over to Jasmine's side of the desk. "Whatever *that* means."

We're still at the paper but have pretty much exhausted all the possibilities here. We know the next thing we need to do is find "the guy with the dagger tattoo."

"You want some help? I can climb a ladder like a billy goat," I tell her.

"No," she says. "They'll put you to work and you'll never be able to leave. When they get into clearing *energy*, things get wacky. Plus, they just got back from that convention, so that means you'd never hear the end of it. I appreciate the offer, but save yourself, trust me."

"Okay."

"And in the meantime," she says, "go home. Get some rest. Relax. We'll handle this tomorrow . . . *together.*"

Jasmine has been so focused on the papers in front of her, she's hardly noticed us, but now she mumbles, "Yes, yes, tomorrow. Let's see each other then."

We leave her bathed in the harsh blue of an overhead neon light, the whole place cleared out except for us. As she pulls out another thick file and pushes the button on her desk kettle, I get the feeling Jasmine won't be leaving this place for hours.

Dally is in Wonderland tonight and looking mighty dapper, like a sight for my sore eyes really. He's chatting with a couple of Legacy girls, and as he passes them their nonalcoholic drinks, he laughs. It's so genuine, so kind and full of bubbly life, I flush at my own suspicions. There's no way Dally has anything intentional to do with anything. There has to be an explanation for the deed to Reflections. I approach him cautiously, grateful for the low lighting and the loud music, which both act like cloaking devices, allowing me to blend in with the crowd. In fact, it's busier than I've ever seen it on a Wednesday. Gary, Dally's right-hand man, is moving at sonic speeds, and there are a few new bodies behind the bar, including one kid who looks like he's just running glasses and bottles back and forth from the kitchen to the bar proper.

Dally stops, midpour, face frozen, rhinestone glasses glittering under the flash of the disco ball. I stop, too, a few feet away, and we watch each other like that, neither of us moving, frozen as the world speeds around us. His eyes are nothing but kind, his lips pursed, frozen in an almost smile I can tell he is holding himself tight to keep emotion in check.

He tears up instantly, lifts his glasses to swipe away any wetness, then opens his arms to me. His minions finish making his drink orders, taking over manning the bar as he comes around.

"Sweetheart!" He scoops me into a hug. He smells like moon-flowers. "Fairy dust, it's been so long. I came to your apartment, you know, but your aunt sent me away. Said you were having a hard time." He squeezes me. "I brought you flowers and some of those sea-salt lilac cookies you like so much."

"I'm sorry, Dally," I say. "I was a mess." I look around. "And I'm sorry about what we did in here."

"Oh, please!" he says. "Look at this place. Business has doubled since the battle. Everyone knows it happened here, so we've been packed with tourists. All my regulars have been in here constantly, too. It's fine. Better than fine! It might be just what I needed." I think again of Dally taking money from Attenborough. There must be a logical explanation. He pauses. "You're the one I'm worried about. And of course I miss seeing James and the boys playing pool, and the dance floor is not the same without Ursula. And"—he leans in conspiratorially—"all this garbage about them being villains. Well, I hate it. I hope they stay wherever they are and never come back. The Scar has turned into a mob scene. They should just wait it out. The Watch won't last forever."

"And you, Dal? How are you doing?"

I don't know if I've ever really asked him about himself. Ever since he opened Wonderland, he's just been this presence, a person I love to see, someone who is a boisterous and fun part of the Scar and who exemplifies what it means to be Legacy.

"Thank you for asking," Dally answers slowly. "I just had to move my mother. She was in that home over on Welsom. I found out they were using the money allotted for health care to give bonuses to the higher-ups. I pulled her out, but it wasn't cheap and I worry about the rest of them."

"Oh, Dally, I'm sorry."

"No, trouble is a part of life. There's *always* trouble. That's why I wear these!" He grins and adjusts his rose-colored glasses. "Now, enough about me—let's go see what the Scar is up to tonight." He wraps his arm through mine, and we stroll through the crowd. He says hello to everyone, asking about each person, hanging on to me as we go. He remembers everyone's name, who their parents are, which classes they're failing, their favorite drinks, their hopes and aspirations for the future, which sports they play, their favorite instruments. Dally moving through Legacy is its own art form.

When we go into the pool room, Dally whispers, "You'll be together again. You really will."

I lean against the pinball croquet machine. My name no longer tops the leader board, something I never would have tolerated a week ago, and now I barely care.

"Dally, can I ask you a question?"

"Of course," he says, waving to someone over my shoulder. "Anything."

"You know the night of the battle?"

"Mm-hmm?"

"There was a tunnel that went from the lab to your back room. Do you know anything about that?"

His face goes blank. "Do you know, that was as much a surprise to me as it was to you. I don't know where that thing came from, and I had it covered over immediately. I think Kyle Attenborough secretly had it put in there so he could sneak people out, but I don't know."

"But wouldn't that be major construction?"

"Well, I'm not here all day long, Mary!" Dally's getting agitated. "They had a false wall put in. It's horrible, but I didn't know anything about it. I'm mortified it happened right under my nose."

"And you've never had any business dealings with Kyle Attenborough? Not ever?"

"Moi?" He points to himself. "And the King of the Narrows? Oh, honey, no. Never. I would never go into business with that man. I certainly wouldn't let him build a tunnel and steal Legacy kids to run experiments on them. They are my children as much as anyone else's." He takes both my hands and looks at me earnestly. "You are my children, you understand? I would never do anything to hurt you."

"Yeah," I say. "Yeah, of course."

He gives me a long, burrowing look. "I miss them, you know?" he says finally.

Not as much as you, though, does he?

I nod because I can't do anything else. No words will come. Any sudden movements might bring on a crying jag. Behind Dally, a new kid I've never seen before takes a shot with his pool cue. All I can think is if James were here, he and the boys would be taking that kid's money. It almost makes me smile.

Almost. Except I can't smile because Dally Star just lied to me. I know he's had business dealings with Kyle, and if they weren't nefarious, he could have just told me about them. I think of the mirror, the deed, Reflections, all the many questions I have for Dally. I remind myself I'm not a detective anymore and my goal is to find out where my friends are. Meanwhile, I just have one question I really want to ask him.

"Dal, have you noticed anyone else acting weird?"

He stands up a little straighter.

"Anyone else?"

"Yeah, like in the last week? Any regulars in here doing anything magical?"

An entire layer of Dally has dropped away, and what is left is scuttling and nervous. "We don't say that word in here."

"Magic?"

"Yes," he stage-whispers. "I don't need trouble from the Watch. And anyway I have no idea who's doing what. You see how many people are in here? I don't know how I'd keep track. And the way the Scar is, with people all over the place, so full of *free spirits* and everything? I don't keep a guest book, if that's what you're asking." His voice is high-pitched and strange.

"Okay, Dally. Sorry for asking."

"No." He softens. "It's okay. It's fine. The Watch just has me on edge. I'd better get back to work. But don't be a stranger, you. Okay?"

"Okay. I won't. I promise."

When Dally goes back to tending bar, I creep down the back stairs to the bathroom. I want to check on the mirror, see if it says anything about Reflections on it or if I was just imagining things again. The walls are painted black and the metal stairs are still creaky and narrow. I hear a noise behind me, but when I check, it's just a girl from the Narrows, trying to get to the bathroom. I don't want to raise any suspicions, so I let her pass me and sneak into the back room instead.

You would never know the secret tunnel had been there. The false wall is real now. There are no openings anywhere. Everything is sealed off. I would have thought Wonderland would be a crime scene, that Monarch PD would have been investigating, maybe there would be yellow caution tape in this area, but there's nothing. It's like they aren't even looking into what happened at all. It's just erased, covered over like it never was.

I hear another noise and jump. I don't want to be in here anymore. There's nothing to look at anyway, and I'm tired of being creeped out. I go into the bathroom just as two Legacy are coming out. One of them seems like she might recognize me, but the other is babbling, so they move past me without too much of a fuss.

Once I'm inside and the noises of the bar are dulled to a thump, I start poking around. There are three mirrors hanging above three separate sinks. The mirrors are pretty standard, just the glass with a black rim, and neither of the first two has anything on the back to mark where they might have come from. I have a little bit of a vertiginous feeling as I approach the third. I remember the night I first saw the girl staring back at me from this mirror, how deranged she looked, her imbalanced smile.

Why not take a look-see?

I check the back of the mirror before I look in it, and there is a small golden sticker that reads REFLECTIONS. Yes, this is the one. This is the mirror I looked in the first night, and I know she'll be there again. She's been waiting for me. I stand in front of the mirror. Take a breath. Open my eyes.

She has on a red leather jacket with a black shirt underneath, and her red hair is piled on her head in a crown of braids and curls. It's my face, but not. My eyes, but not. My eyes don't burn like that. My cheeks are not as rosy, my lips are not as full. It's me, but more of everything.

"Well then?" I say.

Her lips don't move when I speak.

"What do you want?" I demand.

Her mouth parts and reveals teeth streaked in blood.

"Stop trying to scare me," I say. "Where is the Mad Hatter?"

She doesn't answer.

"Where is James? Where's Ursula?"

No response.

"Why are you following me? That's your graffiti, isn't it? You changing the words on the signs, on the TV? Who are you? Why are you messing with me? What do you want?"

I'm yelling in a public restroom, and if anyone came in here, they would think something was really wrong with my mental health, and I'm not sure they'd be mistaken, and right now I don't care at all. This is magic. This is what magic has become now. Infiltration, half-truths, assaults on the mind and spirit. No one is granting wishes anymore. No one is making dreams come true. Only nightmares.

I touch the glass. She pulled me through it once; maybe she'll do it again. Maybe this time she'll give me some answers. She puts her hand up to meet mine in an identical movement.

"Pull me through," I say. "Take me to them."

She smirks.

My hand sits against the cold glass.

"Stop following me," I say when nothing happens. "Leave me alone."

She throws her head back, her throat open to the sky. I can't hear her, but she's laughing. I slap the glass once, twice, and again, but she doesn't stop laughing. She's doubled over now, leaning on the sink in her version of the bathroom.

The door swings open, and a girl with blunt bangs comes in and goes into a bathroom stall. I rush out, not looking behind me, sure if I do, the Red Queen won't be laughing anymore, that she'll be crawling out of the mirror to follow me instead. I make it up the stairs and am a few feet into the main room when I feel someone following me again.

I spin around and find myself face-to-face with Lucas Attenborough.

He snorts, a breathy exhale somewhere between a sigh and a laugh.

He furrows his brow. "Are you okay?"

I glare at him. "Don't do that. Don't you dare look concerned for me."

"Right," he says. "I'm sorry." Someone passes by and I get pushed closer to him. "You weren't at school today, and the last time I saw you, you were getting hauled off by the Watch."

"Thanks to Katy."

"Yeah," he says. "We're not close these days."

"And what about Chase? Surely your pet demons haven't abandoned you."

The look on his face tells me everything, and I let out a laugh. "Maybe there is justice in the world after all."

"Yeah, yeah," he says. "I guess you haven't been keeping up on the news. The *Genie's Lamp* did a big spread about it yesterday. My dad doesn't want anything to do with me, and all of the Narrows has followed."

Lucas freed me. I hate him, but he did let me go. And now his dad won't speak to him because of it?

"You aren't living with your dad?" I ask. I'm reluctant to show I care, but curiosity gets the better of me.

"Nope. My mom." He glances at me, but only briefly. "She's Legacy. Lives above the furniture store on Desire." Wait just a second. Lucas Attenborough is half-Legacy? I'd love to let this sink in and give him never-ending trouble about it, but I'm still too mad.

"Okay, well, thanks for catching me up on your life. Now bye."

"Fair enough," he says. "I have no one now, if that makes you feel better."

"You know, it really does," I say. "You've always been a dick, and now you're getting treated like one. Maybe there's justice in the universe after all. And stop stalking me."

I move to leave, but he stops me.

"Mary, wait," he says. "I think you're in danger. I can help."

I spin on my heels. "Oh yeah? How did you deduce that, you fine detective, you?" I poke his chest. "Of course I'm in danger. Just remember that you're the one who started all this. You're responsible. Stay away from me, understand?"

He puts up his hands in a gesture of surrender.

Satisfied, I leave.

Gia's waiting for me. She's dressed for her day, sitting at the dining room table with her feet tucked under her, and she stands as soon as I walk in.

"The school called," she says.

"Oh." I should be more nervous or feel more guilty, but I have too much on my mind. I take off my jacket and drape it over a chair.

"You didn't tell me what happened with that girl from the Narrows."

"Katy? Not worth mentioning."

"You didn't tell me they banned you from the building."

"No." She gives me a reproachful glance. "No! I should have, but you're already stressed out and it wouldn't have changed anything. I'm still graduating. It's under control."

"Yes, but we have a deal. We communicate with each other."

I twinge and flicker with guilt.

Oh, stop it. It's for her own good, and guilt is for ninnies. Can you imagine what she would do if she knew what you were up to? You'd be shackled to your bedroom door.

"I'm sorry, G, but right now I'm going to have to ask you

to trust me without the communication part. I really need that from you."

"Is that James's jacket?"

I hesitate, but why lie? She already knows the answer. "Yes. I got it when I was at his house."

Gia sighs and rubs her temples.

"I lost my sister, Mary. I also lost my niece, my beloved brother-in-law, magic, my parents, who died of broken hearts."

"You mean my family? Are you trying to remind me of something I could never forget and that you could never possibly understand?"

"I promised your mother if anything ever happened to her, I would take care of you. I promised her I would keep you safe."

"And you are keeping me safe. You *have!*"

"I'm trying, but you make it so difficult sometimes. This city is in turmoil. Kids are Vanishing."

"What are you saying?"

She gives me a pointed look. "I'm saying this is no time for you to be keeping secrets."

"There's only so much I can deal with! I'm doing the best I can. I didn't do anything to get kicked out of school. I didn't choose to get shot up with Wrong Magic. I wish everything would go back to normal. None of this is my fault!" I yell.

"But if you would stay home, exercise some restraint, wait for the detectives on the case to restore some sort of order. At least enough so I don't have to be terrified every time you walk out the door."

I slump into the seat across from hers and take her hand in mine. It's a strong hand, still smooth enough, but beginning to wither. "The truth is, you made a promise to my mother that you can't keep, so you should release yourself from it. I'm sure if she had been able to have coherent thoughts as she died, they would have been about you and how lucky she was to have you there to pick up the pieces."

Gia snuffles loudly.

"But you lied to her when you said you could do that. A million things could happen to me. I could be run over, attacked, murdered like them. I could be stung by a deadly insect or catch an incurable cold."

"But this isn't that. This is you running straight into the fire, your life being pulled apart, you not even getting to finish high school normally."

I meet her eyes. "And that's okay, all of it. I don't care about any of that. *This* is what's happening. I've got to do what I can to help. I'm spending my days well, G. I'm trying to help the Scar, look for an antidote, find James and Urs before the Watch does. I may not be able to do all those things. I may not be able to do *any* of them." I take a shaky breath. "But I will do what I can and you have to let me."

"But you could—"

"Die? Yeah, I guess I could. Everything could also be just fine. And still you have to let me. Because this is my path and this is who I am, and I have to be free to walk it no matter how much it scares you."

She doesn't say anything for a long time, stares into the space between us. I rub my thumb over her knuckle in slow circles, hoping she'll know how much I love her.

"Sometimes," she says after a while, "all the sadnesses stack up so you can hardly see over them. Then it's hard to remember that you can only have sadnesses if you first have love. You go and find your loves, Mary. I'll be all right here."

That was very impressive, She says. *You very nearly had a backbone.*

When I get into my room, I pull my phone out of my pocket and dial. Much as I might have felt confident in the room with Gia, now I'm shrunken, anxious. What I said to her about all the things I'm trying to do made me realize how big it all is, far beyond me.

When I hear Dr. Tink's voice give a perky little "Hello?" I nearly collapse in relief.

TEN

IT'S EARLY FOR THERAPY, BUT IT HAD TO BE EARLY because Tink has to be at her real job at the Monarch City PD at ten o'clock, and meeting there would be awkward at best.

Drive all you want, Mary. You can't escape what's in your own head.

I pull onto a residential block, where the houses are small and run-down, and find a parking spot on the street. Not many cars over here. Boats bob in the water of the bay. This is the most southerly part of the Scar, the end of the line, where the fishermen live side by side with people who would just as soon be left alone as anything. There are no signs here warning of villains and danger, almost like a small, normal neighborhood. I stop and stare into the horizon. It offers nothing, no answers.

I look for the house on the corner of Gossamer and Willowfly with its green roof and brown walls, as described. Like a tree, Dr. Tink said. Then I see her, wrapped in a green sweater and jeans, waving to me from the porch. When I reach her she gives me a short, sharp hug.

"Dr. Tink," I say.

"Tink is good enough for here. Come in, Mary."

Inside, everything is made of wood and creaks pleasantly. The ceilings are low, with viny plants hanging from everywhere. The salt air is in everything, even my muscles, which begin to relax.

"Sit down," she orders. "I'll get you tea."

"Coffee?" I say hopefully, and she makes a clicking noise that tells me it'll be herbal tea and nothing else.

"I'm so glad you reached out to me," she says. "You missed your last appointment, and then there was the battle and all your friends . . . And then you were—"

"Fired—"

"Yes, I suppose you were. Terrible time to stop therapy, though. You're a child, and we were in the middle of some very emotional things."

The last therapy session we had comes back to me in a flash. We had just gone over the last time I saw my sister, the day my parents were murdered, the day I met the chief, who came to help me and promised to catch the killers.

I sink into her sofa, and she hands me tea. It's like all my skin is bruised just under the surface, like I'm a peach, and if someone pressed too hard, I would just explode out everywhere, and so I'm afraid of her questions, that they will be the equivalent of a thumb pushing in all the wrong places.

"So tell me," Dr. Tink says. "What's going on?"

I think about cushioning the reality, telling her half-truths, making myself look more competent than I am, but then I blurt, "Something is really wrong with me. I . . . I need help."

She takes a delicate sip of her tea and tucks a strand of blond hair behind her ear. "Say more."

"I'm seeing things that aren't there, hearing things. And just when I'm convinced I really am delusional, the news confirms some of it."

"Okay, go on."

"Well, for instance, I kept seeing flashes of phrases and then they'd go away, and I'd be the only person who saw them or heard them. Or like, when Caleb Rothco escaped, the woman who helped him was there supposedly at the same time as me, but she couldn't have been. So then I think it's me, I'm going mad, and *then* it's confirmed that all these phrases I'm seeing are actually showing up all over Monarch. It's like someone is getting in my head and bringing it out." My voice wobbles, and I want to strangle myself for my own weakness. "And that's not all."

Tink looks up from her notebook, where she's scribbling. She arches an eyebrow.

"I've been hearing voices."

"Voices?"

"Well . . . a voice."

Tink lets her notebook drop to her lap. "And what does this voice sound like?"

"Me? Me but meaner, more stern . . . It's like she says all the things I wouldn't dare to say."

"Ah. Like your conscience?"

"But louder. She's louder than my own inner voice now. That's not normal."

There it is. The truth. I am not right and I am alone in the world and nothing is ever going to be okay again. I expect Dr. Tink to agree with me, call the authorities, have me hauled away, but she only looks at me with curiosity.

"'Normal,'" she scoffs. "That's just something someone made up. There's no such thing, so just let go of that whole concept." She purses her lips. "Okay. You say the voice began when?"

"A couple of weeks," I say.

"Was there a precipitating event?"

"James—"

She nods knowingly.

"James, I think he had already made contact with Lucas and Kyle Attenborough and had already gotten some of the shots. He gave me some of the magic, or the magic went into me."

"Spontaneously?"

"Yeah. James could make this blue light with his hands, and he . . . I don't know . . . put it into me. Then I started to see her."

"Her?"

"The girl in the mirror."

"Okay, let's start there. What does she look like?"

"The girl in the mirror?"

"Right."

"Well, she looks like me. You know. Shortish, hair like mine but redder, face like mine but more makeup. You know, me . . . but *more* me."

"And what happened to her? Where is she now?"

I never thought of that. I just assumed she was in the mirror and would still be there if I went back to Wonderland. That, or she would be doing other mirror things, living her life like I've been living mine.

But now I'm not so sure. She pulled me through the mirror, but then where did she go until I saw her again? All those things I could suddenly do after she pulled me through. How did that happen? Was it because of the Wrong Magic? No, things were happening before that.

"Tell me what you're thinking," Tink says.

"The night of the battle, I found James and Ursula and Mally because the girl in the mirror pulled me through and I landed in the lab."

"And where was she?"

"I don't know. Gone."

"Okay, and when did you start hearing the voice?"

"I suppose there were whispers before, but it was really when I came through the mirror."

My heart is beginning to thump crazily; the Seed mark on my wrist feels like it's boiling.

"Great ghost," I whisper.

The girl in the mirror, the voice in my head, the Red Queen. "It's me," I say, and even as the words slip from my mouth I see her in my mind, her shining eyes, petulant mouth, tight waist, and cascading red curls. "But how? I don't remember . . . any of it. Not letting Caleb out, graffitiing all over town. How can I be her if she's so separate?" And yet even as I ask the questions, I know none of the logic means anything. I have just spoken the truth, and something huge and violent twists in me.

She doesn't like to be seen.

Tink watches me placidly, unreadable. "How much do you know about magic?"

"I remember magical candies, fairies flying everywhere. Everything seemed possible, everything better."

"Yes, it was all of that. Bright, sparkly, and most of all unpredictable. We've gotten used to the concrete world without magic, where everything has boundaries that can be explained. Anything that falls outside the realm of logic is the fault of the mind. Once you bring magic into it, the whole balance of the equation shifts and changes. Understand? You have to let go of the rules you're familiar with."

"There are no rules?"

"Oh, no," she says. "There are rules all right. They're just different."

"Okay?"

She makes her fingers into a steeple and closes her eyes for a moment as though thinking. "What's your biggest fear, Mary? Quick!"

"Uh . . . having the people I love taken away."

"And has that happened before?"

"Yes, when my family was murdered."

"And is that happening again?"

"Yes, because James and Urs are gone."

"And is any of it in your control?"

"No."

"And how does the Red Queen handle it?"

"She tells me to take revenge, to stand up for myself, to make sure I'm not a victim."

"So what makes her different than any other voice in your head?"

"She can crawl out," I say, and as I do, goose bumps tear across my skin. I picture her climbing out of my mouth while I'm sleeping. "She can separate herself from me. She can get out of the mirror and *do* things. She can make it so I don't even know what I'm doing. She can split me in half. But she can also make me more than I am. She's not scared like me."

"And what James is now, what Mally and Ursula are . . . does that relate in any way?"

I think.

If the rumors are to be believed, Captain Hook is just James but *more*. He's more of a criminal, more of a leader, more in control, more dangerous. Ursula is more of a dealmaker, more of a collector, bigger than she was before. And Mally? She's even colder, even more incisive, even more calculated and powerful. They are all just more. So am I.

So the Red Queen would be more than me, or maybe she's slowly taking over.

The question is, do I want her to? Mary Elizabeth Heart isn't much to look at these days, is she? Kicked out of school, no friends, tired, depressed, powerless, chasing her own tail and accomplishing nothing.

"You okay?" Tink says.

"Yeah."

"What is inside you, what is most core to who you are?"

I think, still trying to process what I think I've just learned. "Me? Love. Loyalty. Anger, maybe?"

"Well, when it comes to magic, what is on the inside is what will come to the outside. It used to be that only the good came out, but I don't think that the good and the bad were ever balanced. Now it's only the negative, or what people perceive to be negative. That's what makes people afraid. It's feral. There is a way for people to be everything they are and have magic and have it work for them. I just don't think we've discovered it yet. And I think when we do, magic will come back to us voluntarily, no tricks."

"But not as the Red Queen?" I say.

"I think the Red Queen is a splinter," Tink says. "The problem with magic is that you aren't in control. Perhaps you can learn—"

"But not in time?"

"And not with the entire city looking for the splintered piece of the self that's totally out of control."

"How is it that you're so calm?"

"Well," Tink says, considering, "ever since magic left when I was a teenager, I've been waiting for it to come back, and now that it's here, I know it won't leave again until things are right. That gives me hope that even though everything seems out of control, magic knows what it's doing."

"But that magic . . . whatever Kyle Attenborough was pushing on my friends that made them into those exaggerated negative pieces of themselves . . . that's not the magic that's going to bring balance to anything. I've got to get rid of it."

Tink furrows her brow. "How?"

"I don't know. Every action has an opposite reaction. There has to be a way."

"Yes, I'm sure there is." Tink stares outside. The ocean laps calmly, and the fishing boats bob up and down in the distance. "I remember when the mermaids used to come hang out on the shore. They've gone below now. I wonder if they'll ever come up again."

"What did you do before you were a therapist?"

She smiles but continues to look outward. "I was a tinker. I come from a long line of them. We fix things, can even build things, only before we used to be able to change sizes. We could get big or small depending on what was needed. I used to have wings. I loved them so much. Then one day I woke up and they were gone."

"I guess you're still tinkering in your own way," I say.

"You think?"

"With people's minds."

She looks at me, surprised. "I never thought of it that way, but I suppose you're right. I do miss my wings, though."

"I hope you get them back someday," I say.

She takes a deep breath, uses her knees for leverage, and stands. "Life is surprising. You never know what it will bring. I suppose that's magic. There are wings in it."

"Thank you," I say. For the first time in weeks, I don't feel like words are folding in on themselves inside me.

"You're welcome." She checks her watch. "You'd better get on, and I have to go to work. You stay in touch. Anytime, anything you need."

"I can't—I don't have any money right now to pay you. I'm so sorry."

"Ah." She waves me off. "Don't you know, Mary? The whole fate of the Scar hangs in the balance. You don't owe me anything. Just do the right thing and remember it doesn't have to be alone."

I get to my feet and charge for the door. There's no time to waste now. There's magic in me, and it turns out I'm not alone at all.

Who says I'm going to help you? the Red Queen says.

Because I see you now, and you're either going to help me or I'll lock us both up where no one will ever find us again.

She doesn't agree, but she doesn't complain, either, and I'll take it. Anyway, I need her to be quiet so I can figure out what to do next. We've got work to do.

ELEVEN

THOUGH MIRACLE LAKE SITS OUTSIDE MY APART-
ment building, I haven't been here since the rally just after the battle.
I've walked around it or behind it or gone mostly the other way. I'm
back here now to meet Lucas Attenborough. I had to grit my teeth
to text him and ask him to meet me here, but if I'm going to get
more information about the source of magic, I'm going to have to
talk to him. Kyle Attenborough's lab is a short walk from here, and
that's where I mean to get Lucas to take me. Maybe there are vials of
Wrong Magic left inside. And if there are, I don't know what to do
next. Go to Gia and the Naturalists, maybe? I'll figure it out once I
get there. For now, I'm just praying someone left something behind.

I'll do my very best not to punch him in the face before I can get
the information I need.

Miracle Lake, which appeared the day after the Great Fall,
when the tallest buildings in the Scar disappeared in a flash of blue
light, is poison. One touch to the rippling water, and whoever is
stupid enough to try is eviscerated instantly. There's only been one
exception that I know of: Ursula, who was in the lake when James
and I found her in her squid form after she'd been missing for
days. She was swimming around in the water like it was the perfect

temperature and an utter delight. I wanted an explanation of how she had accomplished that, but I never got one. Then, when she became a giant and towered over the town, she grew straight from the lake.

I have the explanation now, don't I?

Magic.

Becoming more you than you were before.

If Ursula *were* the poison, she couldn't be hurt by it.

Now Miracle Lake sits in the midday light, half a city block in diameter, shining like a giant coin. If there weren't signs all around the lake warning visitors not to touch the water and railings on the periphery, you would never guess it was such a dangerous place. You would want to go for a swim, row a boat, dip your feet into its waters.

"Heart," Lucas calls. He's in jeans and sneakers and a big white sweatshirt, and he smiles as he approaches.

Seriously?

I hate the sound of his voice and remind myself I'm going to have to be nice to get what I want.

But not too nice.

"What happened to you?" he says. "You look like you've been wrestling a badger."

"Thanks for the compliment." Black jeans, black T-shirt, now James's jacket. This is how I dress. I don't know what Lucas wants from me.

"Just making sure you're okay."

"You're so concerned?"

"I—listen—"

"No." I put up my hands, wave them in his face. "I don't want to talk. Are you willing to take me into the lab or not?"

"Okay, fine," he says mopily. "I was just going to tell you I'm sorry."

My blood heats up. "I know," I say. "I don't want to hear you're sorry. If you're sorry, help me. That's it."

Lucas nods, his cheeks coloring. It's too bad he's such an enormous douche. In another life, he could have been adorable with those little brown waves in his hair, those apple-pie cheeks, and stupid long eyelashes. But no. He ruined it by being a prick. We walk the short distance to the tall building in silence.

"I have a key card for the lab," Lucas says when we get to the door.

"Of course you do. You literally kidnapped people and kept them here. I didn't think you had to break in."

"Yeah," he says.

"I didn't call you because I wanted to hang out."

"Of course not." He scans his card, and the door opens into the lobby. He motions for me to go in.

"Ever the gentleman."

My voice shakes, betraying what I'm trying to hide, a rising pulse, dread at being back here. It's familiar, antiseptic, more like the absence of a smell than a smell in and of itself, like trying to cover up a sickness.

The front desk guy nods Lucas by, and we head silently to the elevator. Our breathing seems loud as the car bullets upward.

"My dad would kill me if he knew I was bringing you here," Lucas says as the doors open. "It would be a billion-dollar betrayal. I've already practically been disowned."

"I'm aware," I say.

He scans his card outside the lab, looks at me sideways. "Are you sure you want to go in?"

"I'm sure," I say. "Just do it."

He pushes a green button, and the doors open.

There are two doors behind the first. One that leads to the hall behind the cages and gives access to them. I look down and see trays, trolleys, and a small kitchen, the actual lab. This is backstage. The other door leads to the hall, where we were the night of the battle. The fronts of the cages. From this vantage point, I can't see each one, but I know there are five of them and that, unless they've been tampered with, one will hold Ursula's water tank and one will be where I was being held.

My body remembers.

Break his neck, the Red Queen says. *Take his head all the way off. Leave it here for his daddy to find. Send a real message.*

I brace myself.

Lucas flips on the lights. "Great ghost," he says.

The lab is a mess. There are empty containers and papers strewn across the floor, open drawers by the control center. All the cabinets have been yanked apart. Someone was in a rage.

We walk farther.

The cages are destroyed, beds shredded, pillows turned inside out, and feathers strewn across the floor.

"The chair," I say.

Shackles and metal cuffs attached to leather straps. A chair for torture and experimentation. The shackles are scattered across the floor, the metal cuffs flattened, the chair itself smashed.

Lucas can't even look at it. He can't look anywhere.

"Where did you keep the Wrong Magic?"

"Is that what you call it?"

"What else?"

"My dad was calling it the Elixir."

"Bit of a euphemism."

"The cops left the samples in some safe. They didn't want them in the evidence locker until they could figure out what they were. They thought they might be unstable, and since there are lab conditions and the place is more or less secured, they would be better off here for now."

Another scan and we're in the hallway behind the cages.

And there's a tear in the wall, jagged-edged, deep, cranky. The opening reveals a refrigerator.

"What the hell?" Lucas says, looking alarmed. But I'm not afraid. James was here.

I can see him ripping papers, tearing up pillows, taking his vengeance on this place. If anything were going to jump out at us, James already took care of it.

Lucas pulls out a key ring. "Before I open this, tell me what you plan to do with them."

"No. I don't have to tell you anything."

"Then no," he says. "You can't push me around forever. At some point, you have to—"

"I hope to find an antidote," I say.

He eyes me skeptically. "You? Are you a scientist?"

"I am the fulcrum," I say.

"Whatever." He grunts, turns the key, scans the card, turns another key, and types in numbers. "My dad," Lucas murmurs. "I went to see him. He's made mistakes," he says.

"Yeah, this was a big one."

"He said he was in danger. That we both were." Lucas opens the door to the refrigerated cabinet as cold air escapes. He gives me a long look. "It's empty."

"You don't say."

"This is bad; like, really bad. This means your friends have gone rogue and have the Elixir with them. They don't know anything about dosage or—"

"Lucas, calm down."

"No! I can't. This is the worst thing that could have happened.

My dad was right. We're all in serious danger now. It's way beyond your boyfriend coming for vengeance. He's messing with something he doesn't understand. We're all screwed. I have to go tell my dad."

He's filling me with anxiety, every word a drop of dread, and if I can't get any of the Wrong Magic, I don't have anywhere to start. I'm back at square one.

Aren't you grumpy? She says.

"I barely had to convince them, you know?" Lucas says, near tears. "I want you to know that. Ursula and Mally and James came of their own free will, sniffing around for magic. When I told them they had the chance to get some, they were all over it."

He's rushing for the door as I struggle to keep up. "Legacy are always blaming the Narrows for everything, but you're all as responsible as we are. Everyone wants magic. They will all do what it takes to get it." The elevator dings, and we jump in it. "You think my dad wanted to give magic to the Scar, that he was making his formula so everything could go back to the way it was? No. The wealthy global community would pay just about anything to be magical. But it didn't work, okay? The non-Legacy literally disintegrated when they tried it."

Kyle tried to give the magic to non-Legacy first. That makes so much sense.

"Why am I even telling you this?" He tears into the lobby and makes for the doors to the outside.

"I have to think," I say to no one in particular. "I just need to think."

Lucas shakes his head. "Yeah, go ahead. Take your time. And meanwhile, someone is running around Monarch with a lot of really, really dangerous magic."

I have so many questions. I know why they would want the magic out of Kyle Attenborough's hands, but there must be something else to it. They aren't just going to keep it in a cooler somewhere and forget about it.

I may not have any answers or know anything of any use at all, but I know someone who does, and I'm going to make her look me in the eyes and have a conversation with me, whether she likes it or not, before this whole situation explodes.

Right. Now.

TWELVE

I TAKE CORNERS TIGHTER THAN I SHOULD, accelerate more than is absolutely necessary. I can hardly help it. The *Sea Devil* urges me to let my foot settle on the gas pedal, to lean into its movements. A pair of mourning doves swoop across my path, then alongside me. I head into the part of the Scar where the buildings are still small and cramped and seem wedged into walls, where colorful washing hangs from window to window, and mopeds line the brick walls.

It takes me a while to find the place I'm looking for as I weave through the narrower streets in the Scar that are mostly cobblestone and were never made for cars. After driving around in circles for a bit, I spot a signboard leaning against the side of a building. At first, it just looks like nothing but a scribble, but the third time I come around, I realize someone has sketched a rudimentary mirror in chalk. I screech into a spot across the street and head in.

REFLECTIONS, the sign hanging over the door reads. It's so small you could never see it from a distance. It seems like the owners are not exactly looking to attract customers. I push through the door with its jangly bell and step down onto creaky wood floor. Dust floats down through shafts of light in languorous spirals. There's an almost-sweet mustiness to the place. The room is littered with stand-up mirrors that all look old and weathered, with wooden frames and metal frames and no frames at all, and the walls are covered in mirrors of every size and shape, ones framed in mother of pearl, silver, gold, complicated beads, in painted wood. There's a mirror in every style, except the one that was at Wonderland. If I'm going to find the girl in the mirror, it will have to be the same one, right? But maybe it's not about finding the same mirror, but rather finding the *magical* mirror.

A *pop* interrupts my train of thought, and I turn to find a girl around my age snapping her gum at me. She's definitely Legacy and is in leather shorts, a white T-shirt, and motorcycle boots. Her hair is black, and hoops climb the side of her left ear. In another life, we might have been friends.

"Wait," she says, clutching a leather-bound door-stopper-size book to her chest. "Are you an actual person in this store, or am I hallucinating?"

She doesn't seem to recognize me at all, so I relax.

"Nope! I'm real," I say. "At least I think I am. Sydney. Sydney Cline."

"Well, shiver me timbers. Blow me down!" She feigns fainting into a pea-green velvet-covered chair in the corner. Then she opens one eye and still slumped over says, "Sorry, it's just I haven't seen a person under eight hundred years old in here since I got this gig. It would appear secondhand mirrors are more of an ancient person's deal."

I grin. "After-school job?"

"Oh, honey, no!" She leaps to her feet. "I graduated a couple years back. Rose." She offers a hand. "Rose Red. And sadly, this is my actual, only job. Overpaid to lounge about, I guess you could say. It's all right. I like reading better than real life anyway."

I offer a hand back. Hers is cool to the touch. "I'm sorry for implying this isn't a serious job. I didn't mean to be a jerk."

"Oh, pshaw! My ego is not fragile. I'm not ever leaving the Scar if I can help it, and I'm not working in Midcity, so this is what's available. I'll take it as long as my stepmonster wants to keep paying me."

"Stepmonster?" I thought Kyle Attenborough owned the place. I know he doesn't have a daughter.

She nods. "She owns the place. Tax write-off or something. It seems boring, right? Tragic even? But it's kind of great. I like to read, old people like to shop for vintage mirrors. It's all good. Still, I must say I'm so deprived of youth it's downright intoxicating. So, what brings you into the crypt today?" Is she lying or does she not know about Kyle? She seems nice enough.

"I recently broke a mirror and need to replace it. I heard this is the best option for something a little off the beaten path. You know, something with a personal touch that didn't come off an assembly line destined for the mall."

"Really? And who pointed you in this direction?"

Jasmine's desk. "Some guy in the record shop? I forget his name. But he seemed to know what he was talking about."

"Yeah, it's been word of mouth forever," she says. "Used to be magic mirrors and all that. It's kind of gone downhill since the Death. You need some help finding one that'll work?"

"No, I think I'll be okay on my own."

"Go to it!" she says. "Prices are on the bottom right." She settles herself into a chair behind the counter and picks up a book that has been lying facedown. "All negotiable," she adds without looking up. "Make me an offer."

"Thank you," I say, pleased to see she's completely distracted by her book, because my Seed mark has started throbbing.

Show me where I can see you. We need to talk.

Maybe I will and maybe I won't. I don't much like taking orders.

My Seed mark heats up, and I feel it, magnetic as it guides me toward the far edge of the store, past the shelves of handheld mirrors inlaid with mother of pearl, made of shining silver, of rippling gold. It stops when I get to a hand mirror that's hanging all the way in the corner. Its frame is made of red wood, and flowers are carved daintily into its edges. The palms of my hands tingle as I approach, my breath is coming fast, and I feel like I'm about to get caught doing something, that the Watch will handcuff me for doing before I can reach it.

It seems like every surface, every bit of glass is waiting for something, leaning toward me, and every molecule whirls at attention. I hear the air go in and out of my lungs, feel my wrist burn so violently I'm sure the skin is bubbling.

The mirror is right at my eye level and is just big enough that I can see my whole head, my hair dripping over my shoulder in waves. I focus on it, on the glass in it, and on making my breathing even. I'm afraid of what I might see, but even more fearful that it will all turn out to be nothing, another disappointment, more hope that leads nowhere.

I let my eyes relax, let myself roll along the bends and curves of my own anxiety until it's smoothed over and dissipates. Running just underneath it is an electric current, faint at first and slow-moving, but then it begins to build, a brilliant, shining buzz that rises from deep inside and pushes from my skin. It's her.

Yes, I think, let me see you.

I let her in a little at a time, and it's an invisible wrestling match as she pushes and I give way, just enough. It's just enough I can feel it pouring from me, radiating, but I'm also straining against her.

The heart on my wrist twists like it's an imperiled animal.

The store drifts into shadow. I hear Rose laugh, but it sounds like it's coming from far away. Time slows its pace as seconds stretch.

Come to me, I think as the power builds. *Come and show yourself to me.*

I expect to find a brutal and intense version of myself staring at me, carved from fury, but instead the mirror goes liquid silver, so I disappear entirely. I train my eyes on its surface, and I know she's coming.

A figure begins to take shape, and I wait for her to come clear. I want to talk to her, to hash all this out. I want us to be friends and help each other.

But it isn't her. The deep eyes and dramatic brows come into focus first, followed by the jawline, the stubble, the short black hair, the olive skin, those perfect, plump lips.

I gasp and reach for the mirror.

His breath goes in and out, the muscles in his neck contract. It's really him.

"James," I whisper.

He smiles. He actually smiles at me, reveals his perfect teeth, and his eyes crinkle with recognition and love. This is *my* James, and there's almost no hint of the madness I saw in him the night of the battle.

"James," I say louder. "Where are you?"

"Hey, baby," he says, the sound of his voice like the grumble of rocks rubbing against one another, like the night sky, like the sound of wolves traveling in shadows. "I'm right here. I'm always right here."

The rubber band holding everything together inside me quivers, and the glass around me trembles, just like my resolve.

"It's hard, isn't it? Fighting all the time?" James says. "Maybe you should just let go."

I trace the surface of the mirror, almost expecting to touch his skin, disappointed by the cold surface. I want to be with him, feel his hand in mine, lay my head into the safest places on his chest. I want to be with him.

"James," I whisper. "I miss you."

"I miss you, too."

"Letting go? Is that how I find you? What does that even mean?"

"I'm sorry, are you saying something?" Rose asks, moving toward me while I try to hold still. "You need some help?"

"I'm fine," I manage, smiling at her. "I'm totally A-okay!" I give her a thumbs-up and turn back to the mirror only to find it empty.

I want to throw myself on the floor and cry like a baby. But I saw him. I saw James.

"I found one I like, so I'm all good!" My voice sounds desperate even to me.

"Oh no! I'm so sorry!" she crows. "Those mirrors in the corner are already spoken for. Just waiting for people to pick them up." She looks panicked, the book beside her forgotten.

My Seed mark thumps so intensely I'm almost sure she can hear it.

"Okay, I'll keep looking." I dust myself off (because there is dust everywhere in this place) and amble over to a midsize mirror with a white frame, still trying to bring myself back to the here and now, still trying not to completely die inside because of fifteen seconds with James Bartholomew.

I keep my face as still as I can and pull the mirror off the wall. "I'll give you forty for this one."

I don't even know what I'm saying.

"Forty, huh?" She looks at it, hands on her hips, then shoots me a smile, looking relieved. "You can have it for twenty."

"Can I have a box?"

"Box?"

"Yeah, something to carry it in?"

"I guess I have a couple lying around in the back." She glances to where the red mirror, *my* mirror, still hangs like it's nothing special, like it isn't the exact thing I need. "Be right back."

She disappears, and as soon as she's out of sight, I dash for the corner, grab my forbidden mirror, and shove it into my backpack. She steps back through the doorway with a cardboard box in hand. "Will this work?"

"Totally."

She packs up the white mirror and seems calm, but her eyes are shifty.

"This is going to look great in my room," I say, needing to fill the space.

"Totes get it," she says. "Need a change every now and then."

The front door swings open just as I'm paying and she's handing me the box. An older man walks in wearing a cloak made of a light cotton with many colors patched together. Rose's demeanor changes in an instant. Her spine straightens, the expression on her face sharpens, and she thrusts her shoulders back.

"Mr. Bolt. How are you today?"

"Rose, my dear," he says, taking absolutely no notice of me, so much so that I wonder if I'm actually here. "I'm going to need one of your *special* mirrors." He lets his gaze go meaningfully to the side of the store where my mirror came from.

"Of course, sir."

"One of my uptown people is dying for one." He reaches into his cloak. "The last was an absolute delight. You said ten thousand?"

Rose blanches and smiles at me.

Mr. Bolt seems to see me for the first time. His expression tightens and puckers, but he doesn't say anything.

"It's been great doing business with you," Rose says meaningfully. "Hope you're happy with your purchase. Bye, Sydney."

"Thanks." I inch past the man, nearly expecting that Rose will stop me at the doorway and demand to see the contents of my bag. I clutch the box and weave around them. Once I'm out the front door, I run.

TEN THOUSAND FOR A SINGLE MIRROR?

If what I stole is worth ten thousand dollars, then what is Rose actually selling? It sure as heck isn't some plain old mirror. I scroll through possibilities. I didn't tell her my real name, or my address, and I paid in cash. If she's doing something illegal, she probably won't call the cops.

I jump into the *Sea Devil* and roll out, mentally apologizing to Rose. I hope she doesn't get in trouble on account of me.

When I get home, I set down the package, sit on the sofa, and unzip my backpack. The apartment is dead quiet because Gia is sleeping, and I pull out the mirror and hold it. The reflection is normal enough. It's just me, looking a little tired and frazzled around the eyes. But it buzzes in my hands.

I saw James, I think. And you're going to help me find out where they are.

Be careful what you wish for, little Mary. Because once I come out for real, there's no telling if you'll be able to put me back.

I shiver, not because she's frightened me, but because after seeing James, feeling him so close to me, I don't know if I want to put her back at all.

THIRTEEN

"BIBBIDI-BOBBIDI-BOO!" I SAY TO THE MIRROR, perched on the dining table across from me. "Mechicka-boo!" I hover over it, making complicated movements with my fingers. "Do *something*!" I threaten.

This is the most anticlimactic moment of my life. It's like getting the most coveted toy on the market and then finding it doesn't do any of the things it claimed in the commercial.

Gia's sleeping, so I'm trying to be quiet, but I want to scream.

So, what? How? Do I have to be in Reflections to make the mirror magical? Do I have to be in a certain mood, a particular emotional state? Does the mirror have to face a certain direction, be hanging on a wall at a certain angle?

"Be magic!" I command. "Come on, mirror, old pal. Bring me the Red Queen." If it won't work outside of the store, then I'm stuck following Jasmine and Bella around and hoping that trailing the money in all this leads me somewhere.

The mirror glass stares at me.

"What was that in the store, you little faker," I say, poking my reflection in the chin, carefully tapping the glass. "You're a real disappointment, you know that? I have a good mind to smash you into a million little pieces and throw your remains right into Miracle Lake." I pick it up, walk right over to the bin, and hold it over the garbage. "You can go right on in there with the banana peels and the coffee grounds."

But I can't do it. I just can't. Instead, I take it back to the table and set it down among the pink tissue papers and the boxes of Aunt Gia's products.

"What are you looking at?" I demand of my reflection finally. "You just going to stare at me all day? Nothing to say for yourself?"

There's no answer. Nothing.

I think of James, my mind drifting again to thoughts of him wrapping his arms around my waist, his face hovering over me. I let my eyes lose focus. The mirror begins to swim before me, the hard reflection transforms into vapor. I try not to cling to anything, not to sharpen any of my edges, to just let this be what it is.

"Magic mirror on my table," my voice slides out, "find me James Bartholomew if you're able."

The mirror shudders.

The Red Queen swims her way to the top.

The mirror glass falls away, dissolves, and where I should see myself there are only shadows.

"Aren't you a treat?" I hear.

That's Maleficent. I'd know her cold, hard voice anywhere.

A wing flaps across the surface of the glass. Her bird, Hellion. My heart picks up speed.

"Do my bidding." I don't even know this voice coming out of me, but the mirror seems to be afraid of it or something, because the image on the other side gets clearer. "Show me where they are."

It's hazy, a glinting flash, nothing more.

"What was that?" I say. "Show me."

A hook, its sharp edge pressing into the other side of the mirror. It scrapes along the surface.

I tower over the glass.

"Make yourself bigger," I say.

Blue light roils across the mirror's surface like lightning, static, a brewing electrical storm. The glass elongates, stretches. My mouth is dry, but I also feel something new surging inside me. The voice. Her voice. *My* voice.

The mirror stops contorting when it hits the ceiling. It's massive now, eight feet, with its rose frame and ornate decorations. I caress it, fingers crackling, and I love it. Really love it. It's like a buttery pair of shoes, a fuzzy sweater, a T-shirt made of soft combed cotton. It's mine. I let my fingertip graze the glass.

"Take me to my friends," I say.

I push a finger into the glass, and sure enough, my finger connects to the sharp end of the hook, a prick of pain surging through me. I push a little harder and get ready to try a foot, but instead of passing through the glass as I planned, I scream from white, raging, burning pain that tears through my flesh so it bubbles and boils.

This is her.

This is what it feels like to have her completely take over. She clouds my eyes, invades my heart, contorts all of my thoughts until I am nothing but pain. There is nothing left of Mary Elizabeth Heart but anger, and the anger is enough to blow my entire neighborhood apart.

No. I don't want this. I take it back. I want to be Mary again. Just Mary.

But She pushes back.

Everything that has happened to me in this unlucky life spirals through my mind: my parents and sister being murdered, witnessing the Fall, losing all my friends, poverty, living when there has been no magic. I want to tear everything on this planet to shreds. I want to make everyone who has ever hurt me pay. I open my mouth to scream again, because holding this in is too much for me and I can't bear it for another second, but before I can get my voice to leave my throat, the world goes dark.

I come to in my bedroom, lying flat on my back on my bed, cocooned in my satin blanket. The light has changed. It's not afternoon anymore. My green reading lamp is on. The window is open, and a breeze cools my cheeks. My head pounds. I try to sit up, which is when I realize I am tied to the bed with the pink nylon cords Gia uses to send her packages.

"Gia!" I call.

She rushes in, swaddled in her robe, eyes red and darting about. "Mary?"

"Yes, it's me!" I squirm and then go limp. "Why am I tied up?"

"What were your favorite shoes when you were little?"

"What?"

"You heard me. Your shoes. What shoes did you wear until they gave you blisters and curled your toes?"

"My red boots?"

Gia's face drops with relief. "Oh, thank pixies. Are you all right?"

I twist again, and she approaches me, carefully. She lifts her arm, and the sleeve of her robe falls away, revealing her pale, freckled skin, slashed with red marks. Deep welts.

"What happened to you?" I try to sit up but can't.

"You really don't remember?" she murmurs.

"Did I do that to you?" I ask. "Auntie G?"

She loosens the bonds. I sit up, rubbing my numbed arms, and she slumps onto the bed. "It was like it wasn't even you," she says. "I walked into the living room to ask you if you wanted some coffee. I was planning to talk to you about a schedule for homeschooling because you can't be going around all over the place without some kind of structure. You need study hours. When I was your age, I was out carousing at all hours—"

"G!"

"Right, right." She fusses with the bedclothes. "I tried to ask if you were okay and I touched you and you . . . well." She shows me her right arm, which is still bloody and torn.

"I attacked you?"

She squirms uncomfortably.

"Tell me."

"Your shoulders got quite straight. You threw them back actually and then you sort of swished—"

"Swished?"

"Swished over to the drawer and got a knife."

"A knife?"

"Are you just going to repeat everything I say?"

"Sorry. Go ahead."

"You told me you were going to find the chief and—"

"What?"

"You looked right at me. You said that she's lying to everyone. You told me you've had enough of her trying to be in charge of everyone and she doesn't deserve the head that sits on her shoulders. You said heads will roll and it's time to be off with her head."

"And then?"

"I tried to take the knife, and you slashed me with your fingernails." She pulls her knees in closer. "Twice."

I feel the blood in my body, each droplet its own nerve ending buzzing through me as it rips through the thoroughfares of veins and arteries. I'm full to the brim, coursing with *her*.

Stand down, I think.

Only because I kind of like this aunt of yours. So spunky.

"And then you passed out," Gia goes on, shrugging. "Fainted or something. The knife went flying, and I dragged you into bed." She looks to the rope. "I'm sorry, I didn't know what else to do."

"Wrapped me up like a pretty little package," I say.

"Yeah, I didn't know which version of you would be there when you woke up. I didn't know if I should call a doctor, take you to the hospital, or what. With the Watch and everything, I wasn't sure." She hesitates. "It felt like . . ."

"Magic."

"You did seem enchanted," she admits. "Even your voice was different. You were so calm about potential murder. Seems like if you were going to have at the chief and it was you, you'd get a little bit excited at least."

We laugh, but it's uncomfortable and hollow and fills the room with hesitation and fear. Because it's true. I wouldn't calmly talk about taking a butcher knife to someone's neck. I would only use a knife in a violent way if I were defending myself in a life-or-death situation. I am not a predator, even if the chief really, really deserves to be taken off her pedestal.

It's thoughts like that, new, violent . . . Are they mine or are they hers?

Ours, she says. *Wouldn't you like to be a queen, Mary, instead of a chittering little mouse, afraid of her own shadow?*

"Did you say something?" Gia says.

"It's just . . . I've been seeing this graffiti that says that stuff. The things I said to you, I mean. I saw it on the news once and on a sign at the rally the other day. I don't know . . . maybe it got into my subconscious or something, and then something happened that set me off and I repeated all the things I had seen?"

"Hmm." Gia looks at me, head tilted.

"Hmm? Is that all you have to say?"

Gia smiles sadly. "You look like your mom . . . like me, I guess."

I don't know what to say. I look at our hands, twins, hers older and more weathered, but the shapes of our fingers, our nail beds the same.

"It's still so sad, honey, for me. What happened to your mom, your dad. I used to be plagued by visions of their final moments. And Mira?" Her lip quivers. "I still can't allow myself to go too deep into it or I go right back into the place where I was after. It wasn't good." Her eyes are wet. "And you had to deal with all of it."

"I don't remember," I say, even though I do.

"I wasn't really there for you. I was too busy going through my own pain. It was so soon after the Death, my business had fallen apart, and I had this girlfriend who I totally thought was the love of my life and then it turned out she was seeing this guy from the Narrows, which was the worst. I had never felt so—"

"Empty," I say. This is how grief works. You're searching for something to fill up your hollow bones and wet your throat so you can speak, so you can feel anything but all the vacancies inside. And then in a wave . . . *whoosh* . . . you're full, too full, you're drowning and you can't swallow all the water, all the feelings. There's not enough of you to withstand it. "Or full."

"Yeah. I was so tired from holding up the universe. I wish I'd given myself some time to feel my feelings and fall apart."

"But you had a kid all of a sudden."

"Oh, honey, you didn't ask for anything. You drew pictures and played by yourself. It took a long time for you to open up to me, and I let you exist like that. I should have taken us both to therapy. I should have given us the chance to process, and I should have asked you how you were feeling. You should never have had to keep all that bottled up."

I have three memories I go back to again and again from the time around the death of my family. One, the day of, when my mother took me to school. Two, the evening of, when I was at the station and the chief came to take care of me. Three, the press conference when Ito solved the murder and it was announced to Monarch that she would be promoted to chief of police.

"I think you can hold all that alone for a long time," Gia says, "but not forever. At some point, it's going to come back and demand your attention. I've been missing my sister so much." She lets out a dry laugh. "What I wouldn't give to hear one of her annoying rants, to fight with her in the kitchen about . . . I don't know, anything." She shrugs. "I don't have any answers. Just questions. But I do know you need rest." She holds my hands in hers and looks me straight in the eyes. "Can you give yourself the time to rest now? James and Urs are gone, you're not in school, and we might have money coming . . . real money."

"What?"

"Well, I was going to tell you . . . I don't know . . . I don't want to stress you out."

"I'm fine. I feel perfectly normal. Tell me."

"I was contacted earlier today by an investment group. They want to buy some property in the area surrounding Miracle Lake, and this building is one of the spaces. They offered us a lot of money, Mary." She grins. "I mean, a *lot*."

Alarm bells are clanging so loudly I can hardly hear my own thoughts. "Who was it?" I ask, trying to keep my voice steady and not change my posture.

She furrows her brow. "Well, it wasn't anyone from the Narrows, if that's what you're worried about. I would never sell to uptown."

"Then who?"

"I thought you'd be happy, actually."

"Who, G?" I grit my teeth.

"Jack Saint," she says, in a singsongy voice. She doesn't seem to see the jolt that passes through me. Lightning. "I'm not saying I'm going to take it," she goes on. "This apartment has been in our family for a long time, and of course they've done all those studies about what happens to Legacy when they're away from the vortex. If magic ever did fully come back as it was, we wouldn't have it if we weren't in Monarch. And of course the Naturalists would be devastated if I let go of this property. It's a tradition for us to meet here, but I don't know.... The Scar has become so oppressive. Maybe we could give it some thought?"

I can't focus. I can't focus at all.

"Imagine," she says dreamily, "we could go somewhere warm by the beach. Buy a little house. You could finish your senior year remotely, and we could get some space from all this, determine what we want to do next."

"If we sold, we could never afford to come back here. The way prices have gone up ... that would be it."

Gia nods. "Yeah, you're right. I would have enough cash from the apartment sale to start my own cosmetics company. We'll always be Legacy, which lends us a little ... mystique out in the real world." She stands up. "Anyway, now's not the time to talk about it. Jack gave me a few days to decide."

"A few *days*?"

"We can talk when you've gotten some sleep and those bruised lids have gone back to their normal color."

"Okay." I yawn. "You're right. I'm really tired. Need some sleep. I'll feel right as rain in the morning, I'm sure."

"Yeah." She looks relieved and pats me on the leg. "I'll go make you some merrypetal tea. It'll help you sleep."

"No thanks. I'm really wiped out."

She looks at me a beat too long before stretching tall, so I hear a few joints pop. "It's no fun getting old." She leaves but then comes back right away, the mirror, once again its original size, in hand. She lets it drop on the bed next to me. "I found this in the living room. I assume it's yours?"

"Mm-hmm." I try to sound nonchalant. "Thanks."

"It's cute. Reminds me of the magic one I had when I was a little girl. In addition to our talent with beauty, the family was extraordinary at portal magic."

I stare at her. This is turning out to be the most illuminating conversation I've ever had with my dear aunt Gia.

"You didn't know?" Gia says. "Oh yeah. We were fabulous. Could go just about anywhere if we had the right doorway, and there's no better portal than a mirror, if you ask me." She sighs. "If only it were the good old days. Your mother and I had a time before she turned against the family's magic. We surely did." She chuckles as she goes.

So many pieces have just connected for me, I'm struggling to catch up. My mother, portal magic, Jack Saint, our apartment, real estate surrounding Miracle Lake, mirrors, Miracle Lake, Miracle Lake, Miracle Lake, Miracle Lake. There's something I'm still not getting, like a word I can't remember that's so obvious I can't see it.

I can't do this on my own. It's time for me to assemble Monarch's crack team of rogue detectives.

FOURTEEN

IT WAS BELLA'S BRILLIANT IDEA TO GO TO THE public-records office in Midcity bright and early Friday morning. Her jaw dropped to the floor when I told her about Jack Saint offering to buy my apartment, and I've been able to see the actual wheels turning in her brain ever since. She's in an extra-special Midcity outfit: a sweater dress, trench coat, a Lucci bag on her shoulder, and reflective aviator sunglasses hiding her eyes.

"You could have at least made an effort," she says. "What if we're recognized?"

"You think that getup is going to fool anyone? Your perkiness is brighter than any fashion atrocity you can think up."

"Well, that's just uncalled for," she says, hugging the side of the building.

The public-records office is directly across the street from the police station, which Bella has been watching as though gargoyles are going to descend from the facade at any second, pluck her up in their talons, and deliver her to the chief.

"Why don't you read a book or something?" I say. "You like those, right?"

Bella taps her ear. "I'm listening to one right now."

The chief's window is just a few stories up. I wonder what she's doing in there. Probably chewing on the heart of a virgin or something. She wouldn't be able to see me from her vantage point, but I feel her eyes on me anyway. Creepy, narcissistic, psychopathic—

"Mary! Jasmine's coming!" Bella grabs me, and we run over to meet Jasmine, who is leaving the building, stuffing an envelope into her blue leather jacket. She zips it up and walks at a rapid pace, checking behind her as she goes. She passes by us, her heels clacking loudly against the concrete, and says, "Not here. Get on the train."

Bella and I look at each other and then scurry to the subway after her. There's no Watch here, but all three of us are too tense to talk. We use our passes, the gates open, and we get on the train silently. Jasmine doesn't look at us, and we don't look at her. I want to tell them they're being idiots. Our passes could be tracked, and if anyone wanted to know where we are, our phones are literal tracking devices anyway, but I let them do their thing. It's very detective/reporter, and I have to admit my stomach is all twisted up.

When we get to the *Genie's Lamp* offices and huddle in Jasmine's cubicle, Bella can't take it anymore. "What did you find?" she bubbles. "Tell us!"

Jasmine unzips her jacket, rips open a manila envelope, and pulls out a deed. Bella and I both go for it at the same time and end up knocking our foreheads together. I'm so eager to see what's written on it, I don't even care.

Bella sucks in her breath, tucks a pin curl behind one ear.

"Saintly Solutions has *bought* Miracle Lake . . ." I say.

"From the Attenborough Conglomerate," Bella finishes.

"Damn," Jasmine says, breathless as she leans against her cubicle and stares into space. "Wouldn't you love to have been a pixie on that wall?"

"How badly do you think Jack Saint bullied Kyle Attenborough to make that deal?" Bella asks.

"He paid a hundred million dollars for it," Jasmine says, thrusting another document at me.

I let out a little squeal at the amount written on it.

"It's like Monopoly money."

"I've never heard you make that noise before, and I hope I never hear it again," Bella says. "Truly disturbing."

I page through the documents, my heart pounding. "Shut up," I say, "and look at this."

Bella takes the papers, and her expression tells me she's making the same connections I am. Jack Saint now *owns* Miracle Lake, the landmark that came into existence when the tallest building in the Scar disappeared in a flash of blue. He also owns the building that housed Kyle Attenborough's now-deserted lab, and three other buildings surrounding the lake.

"Look!" Jasmine says, handing over the last document in her pile of treasure. "This was just filed yesterday. Saintly Solutions has just become the majority shareholder in Wonderland."

"Jack Saint bought Dally out?" I say, trying to get a better look.

I would very much like to snatch the paper out of Jasmine's hands, but instead I try to angle my head so I can see.

"Keep your voice down," Bella hisses, "unless you want this on the news tonight."

"Hell no!" Jasmine says. "This is my story. No one's going to scoop me."

"Wait, am I seeing this right?" I whisper.

"Yeah, you are," Bella says, pursing her lips in disapproval. "Jack Saint didn't buy Dally out. They're partners now. Dally, Jack Saint, and the chief." She swipes her index finger in a triangle, as if connecting the three of them on her mind map. "And why do you suppose that would be?"

I have ideas now. Lots of them forming like a tornado, rolling and spinning around me. And now I know one thing for sure: The only building Jack Saint doesn't own in the entire area that surrounds Miracle Lake is mine.

What is he planning?

I tell them I have to go home to Gia. I tell them I forgot about an appointment to get my teeth cleaned. I tell them I left laundry in the washing machine. I can't stop making excuses for why I have to leave as I back out the door. Bella and Jasmine have theories.

Jack Saint is going to start a renovation project in the Scar.

Jack Saint is going to emerge as the new hero of the Scar. He's got something up his sleeve, and there's a grander vision behind all of this.

This is an area of the Scar that was beginning to be taken over by the Narrows when the Great Fall happened, so now Jack Saint is going to restore the balance to get magic to come back.

But my mind is whirring with just one thing.

Maleficent.

Maleficent.

Maleficent.

I can almost hear the Red Queen laughing. She's not saying anything, only cackling joyfully, like I've finally gotten something she's been trying to tell me all along but that I've been too stupid to understand. I know very little about Mally's dad, Jack Saint. I know that he only loves two things: his wife, who died in the Fall, for which he blamed Kyle Attenborough. And his daughter, Mally—Maleficent. I don't believe he would do a single thing, not one, without having her in mind. When she was missing and we all thought she was dead, he was so wounded and devastated he looked like a twisted tree, a beaten bloody heart nailed to its trunk. Then to have Mally come back in the way she did, to be released from her cage with new horns protruding from her head, only to wage such a public battle and then disappear? It must have given him new energy to know she was alive. It must have given him new purpose.

I'm rolling closer and closer to my block when the last piece of the puzzle clicks into place.

Jack Saint knows where his daughter is. It's the only thing that makes sense. And if he knows where Mally is, he knows where James is, and he knows where Ursula is, too. And now so do I.

He's not trying to start a renovation project surrounding Miracle Lake.

He's trying to protect it.

I pull into a parking spot at Miracle. So much has happened here: the Great Fall; the deaths of thousands of people; Ursula, emerging from the dark water surrounded by tentacles; the Battle of Miracle Lake; the Fear the Villains rally. We can't escape it. It pulls us to it. We all orbit its dangerous waters. How could I not have seen this sooner?

Miracle Lake is the beating, wounded heart of the Scar.

Miracle Lake is the center of the vortex.

Are you going to keep fighting it, or let it pull you in?

I open my mouth to tell her to shut up, then think better of it. I need her help.

The excellent thing about all the crappy weather the Scar has been having lately is that there aren't the usual suspects out on lounge chairs sunning themselves, and no one is on the grass or anything. The yellow incandescent floating paper lanterns are still bobbling around the lake, but other than that, I don't see anyone around. There are no rallies or protests today. Everyone's taken the warnings about the Vanished seriously and is abiding by the curfew. No one is around to see what I'm about to do.

And what I'm going to do, exactly, is what my aunt and mother and all the women in my family have done for generations: find a portal, and go through it.

I stare out at the placid, reflective surface of this poisonous lake and wonder if I'm looking at one giant mirror. Could Miracle Lake be a super-portal?

Here's what I know. Jack Saint bought this lake and all of the surrounding property, maybe, just maybe, because he has the same theory I do. That this lake will lead us to the villains.

I know Bella would object to this detective work. My evidence is circumstantial at best; at worst, a hunch.

And yet.

And yet I can't escape Miracle Lake's gravitational pull. My body lurches toward the water until I have to brace myself on the protective railing.

"Hey!" I screech.

My voice echoes out, and the tug of the water intensifies until my torso bends over the railing. I grab hold of it as hard as I can and brace my feet, my heart racing. People disintegrate when they touch Miracle Lake. I've seen the footage with my own eyes. My wrist burns madly, my Legacy heart thudding, so I'm pretty sure it's about to burst open and blood will spray out everywhere. That'll be the end of me, and all because my tainted-magic-dosed Legacy heart wanted to become one with Miracle Lake.

Shhhhhh, I hear.

But this is not her. This weaves through me, snakelike, and shakes me at my core.

Magic mirror, first of them all,
Show her the reflection,
Let Mary hear the call.

The voice comes from everywhere, a preternatural command that makes the trees shake, the metal vibrate under my hands and feet, and a fissure appear in the concrete beside me. I hold strong and turn my eyes back to the water, really understanding now.

Miracle Lake *is* a mirror. The water is so shiny, so reflective that I can't even see what's beneath its surface. No one has been able to do any research as to what's beneath it because it literally murders anyone who would try. It occurs to me that somehow the ten-thousand-dollar mirrors in the corner of Reflections, could be made from water out of Miracle Lake. I wonder if Jack Saint has figured out a way to touch the water, to interact with it without getting himself killed.

Before I can think through anything else, the lake shimmers. It's not my face anymore, looking back at me, terrified and contorted. In fact, it's not a mirrored surface at all, but a dark gray expanse, the color of a stormy sea. I focus, every bit of me on high alert, and then a tentacle sweeps the surface of the water, and I almost whoop out loud.

Ursula!

I let go of the railing to clamp both hands over my mouth. The water doesn't suck me in or drown me. The magnetic pull has calmed.

A skull-and-crossbones flag flutters across the water, and then a glinting silver hook trails just below me.

I reach for it, for James, but just before I have the chance to touch it, I'm yanked backward.

"What in pixie dust are you *doing*?" Bella yells.

I ball my fists and mean to throw a punch, but then I see the look on her face.

"You were going to die, Mary!" she screams. "You were going to touch Miracle Lake!"

How could she know? I wasn't going to die. The lake wouldn't let me. My friends wouldn't let me. I slow my breathing, try to make the violent anger dim.

"You followed me," I say.

"You were acting so strange. I wanted to make sure you were okay, which clearly you're not."

"I don't know, Bella. Maybe I'm better than I have been in a long, long time."

FIFTEEN

"WELL?" BELLA IS LITERALLY TAPPING HER TOE at me. "Are you going to tell me what that means?"

I'm still trying to recover myself and not let her see that I'm shaking, as much with excitement over my discovery as the fact that I almost hurled myself into deadly water and was possibly seconds away from perishing.

She fishes around in her purse and comes away with a chocolate chip protein bar. "Here." She slaps it into my hand. "You need to eat."

She's right, and I'm even more grateful when she follows up with a small bottle of water. When I've got myself back together, I say, "It wasn't going to kill me, okay? I wasn't going to die."

She squints at me, making that face she does when she's trying to see into the depths of my soul, which thank all the fairies she can't. "Okay," she says finally, satisfied by whatever she's found. "I believe that *you* believe that. But, Mary—"

"I saw something," I say, internally asking for forgiveness for my lie of omission.

"In the lake?"

"I thought I did," I amend.

"What? Like a fish?"

"No. It was just my own face. But for a second, I couldn't tell. I leaned too far over."

Bella sniffs at nothing in particular. "I don't like it. Every time I come here, my Seed mark acts strange and I feel like I could just plunge myself right in there. With everything that's going on, the last thing I need is some lake tricking my eyes."

"What if it's not tricking your eyes?"

"Meaning . . . ?"

"Oh my gosh! We are not just this." I pinch her.

"Ow!"

"We aren't just flesh and blood. We're magic, too, and we should stop trying to fit into a world that isn't made for us. We're Legacy. We can make things better, take care of all the things we care about, but not if we're acting like weaklings. We need to be the wolves we are!"

"Magic is dead," Bella says automatically.

"No, it isn't!" I yell. "It's not dead at all, and it never was. It's in all of us. All of us have Traces of magic. All of us have Seed markings. All of us are Legacy. Enough of trying to conform. Enough of trying to make ourselves small. We are not small. We are *special,* Bella, *powerful,* and the sooner you figure that out, the sooner you'll stop playing the game *they* set up for us and start figuring out that we have to *invent* a whole new game."

Bella looks confused. "But . . . we have to play by the rules to some extent. Otherwise you're talking about . . . anarchy."

"Maybe in the short term, yeah. Maybe that is what I'm saying. Society is not working out, the people in charge are all crooked. Maybe it's time to take the whole thing apart and start something new."

"Who's going to do that, eh, Mary?"

"Us. We will."

"Us? You mean us, including the villains?"

"Yes! No! I don't know . . . Maybe. And we have Jack Saint on our side, too."

"Jack Saint?" She erupts into laughter. "He's a businessman just like the rest of them. You can't possibly expect him to behave ethically."

"Come on, Bella. You met him," I say. "Think about it. He's Legacy, not just another big-shot Narrows real estate mogul trying to gentrify the Scar. He's one of us. Doesn't it make more sense that he wants to protect us, not further tear down our home?"

"Us?" Bella says again, with a tremor in her voice.

"Yeah. All of us. Legacy. The Scar. Us."

She lays a hand on my shoulder and looks at me gravely. "When are you going to stop putting people on pedestals?" she asks. "I wish it weren't true, but everyone is out for themself. If Jack Saint is buying up the Scar, it's because he's going to make money or he has something major to gain from it.

"And," Bella goes on softly, "it doesn't matter if we have really good intuitions or not. In order to know for sure if we're right about something, and in order for Jasmine to expose the truth about what's happening here and what happened to your friends, we need proof. Concrete, irrefutable proof. That's it. End of story."

"End of story," I repeat, feeling dizzy now, and stupid and childish for everything I said to her.

"I really hope you're okay. You should get some rest. Jasmine found the guy with the dagger tattoo. His name is Trent McCutcheon, and he's agreed to meet with us tomorrow morning. Well, he agreed to meet *her*, but we're going to tag along. I would *like* to take you with me. But you have got to be professional and calm, and you have got to get your priorities straight. You want to invent the game? Jasmine is our path to it. Through real journalism, logic, research, diligence, and vetted data. That's it, Mary. I know you feel passionately about so many things. I do, too. But you can't let the passion control you. You'll never win that way."

My cheeks flush. My throat swells.

The thing is, I know I'm right. Everything Bella said may be true, but that doesn't mean everything I said isn't. That only leaves me with one thing to do.

Prove it.

The landing at Jack Saint's apartment has been totally taken over. As I crane my neck past security and up the staircase, I still see golden ravens carved everywhere and the sculptures of them on every knob and railing. Half a dozen men and women stand in my way. These aren't Watch, either. No gray suits. They're all in black T-shirts and pants, with radios attached to their shoulders, and they're holstered to the max. I immediately clock at least three guns on each of them.

"I'd like to see Jack Saint," I say as pleasantly as possible.

"Name," a man with neatly cropped black hair says.

"Uh . . . Mary Heart?"

"Relationship?"

"Friend of his daughter's . . . I guess."

"You guess?"

"It's complicated," I say, hating how much like a teenager I sound. He's throwing me off my game. I don't know why, but his stern gaze is making me feel compelled to explain that Mally and I have never actually been that close and I never really liked her, if I'm being honest; that I'm not totally sure, but it kind of seemed like she maybe had the hots for my boyfriend and yet we had some kind of psychic connection while she was being experimented on, so now I have kind of a soft spot for her.

"Pat her down," he says.

A woman gives me a thorough once-over. "Clear," she says.

"Good," the man answers.

We wait in total silence for more than a minute, and I am being completely serious when I say the man never for a second takes his eyes off me. I don't know what to do with my hands or feet at all whatsoever.

There's a beep, and the man says, "You can go up."

I try not to run, but when I get to the steps, I take them two at a time.

I practically fall into Magda's arms when she opens the door. She's a salty elderly maid of Jack's, but she's a whole lot warmer than the situation downstairs. I'm dearly happy to see that she has the same scowl and the same white bun tucked into the nape of her neck that she had the last time I was here. She hasn't changed at all, and she may be the only thing that hasn't.

"I know," she says, wiping her hands roughly on her apron. "Don't even tell me nothing. I have already told Mr. Saint that just because he is a big shot now he doesn't need to hire strangers. Anton and I can take care of everything. But"—she shrugs—"he doesn't listen to me, so what can I do? Now you have to get patted down, and Anton—all he does is nap and drink and nap and drink and nap and drink." She throws up her hands. "Well, what are you waiting for? Bring yourself inside."

Once again, I'm struck by my own poverty as soon as I cross the threshold. The room is beautiful, pristine, every detail realized to perfection. I take in the thoughtfully placed modern art, the antique carpets, the objects scattered here and there that must be worth hundreds of thousands. I should probably have to take some sort of detoxifying steam shower before I'm allowed in here. And, wow, am I ever a mess. Little bits of protein bar cling to my hoodie, I haven't changed my clothes in two days.

Jack Saint doesn't seem to care. When Magda guides me into his office, a part of the apartment I've never seen before, he rises from his seat with a huge smile on his face and his arms outstretched while I'm still yards away.

"Mary Elizabeth Heart." He reaches me and embraces me. He smells like pipe tobacco and something green and sharp. Gone are the deep furrows of worry. He looks like he's eaten some, too, where he was so gaunt and hunched the last time we met when he thought his daughter might be dead.

I'm so relieved to be in his arms even for a second. A father. A parent. Someone who loves the people who are being hunted as much as I do. We're on the same side. He stands back and holds me by the shoulders, looking me up and down like he's making sure I'm all in one piece.

"Good," he says. "Excellent." I might be making it up, but his eyes even seem a little watery. "Have a seat, please. Magda, bring us some tea and some of those lovely little cookies you made yesterday."

"Yes, Mr. Saint." She disappears silently.

Only then do I really look around his office. There are no photographs on the wall, only a couple of paintings, slashes of dark lines on white canvas. The windows are open, and the ravens flutter in and out past gauzy curtains and climb on iron contraptions that line the floor behind Jack's desk. Even as he takes his seat across from me and as I slump into a buttery black leather chair, three black birds descend behind him and use their clawed feet to maneuver back and forth until they finally stop and train their eyes on me. I can only imagine what it would be like to be his enemy, stuck in some business meeting with him and all those birds who look like they could rip you apart with sharp beaks if you said the wrong thing.

"They're so badass," I say when one readjusts its wings.

Jack Saint chuckles. "They really are." He folds his fingers into a steeple on his desk and leans forward. "So what can I do for you? You caught me at an excellent moment, and I am truly, truly happy to see you. There are so few people who can understand what we've gone through, all the misinformation being spread."

"Exactly!" I say. "It's like they don't even see what happened, like no one understands they were victims."

"The operative word being *were*," Jack says.

I'm about to ask him what that means when Magda comes back with a gold tray and serves us tea.

"Sugar?" she asks.

"Yes."

"Yes, what?"

"Yes . . . please?"

"Good. Cream?"

"I can do it myself."

"Nonsense."

"Okay, yes, then. Yes, please."

"Good."

She deposits two cookies covered in powdered sugar on the plate in front of me and does the same for Jack and then leaves.

"Vanillekipferl," Jack says. "Delightful."

"Mmm," I say. I take a sip of tea, but my mouth is still dry. It suddenly seems so ridiculous that I would be here with Jack Saint, the richest Legacy in the Scar, demanding to know his business plans. I probably need to check myself. But then I remember what Bella said about getting proof, and then I think crazier things have happened than people just being honest with each other. Maybe he won't be horribly offended and have his ravens peck me apart for dinner.

Somehow Jack manages to eat a bite of powdered sugar cookie

without getting sugar anywhere, while I add a spray of powder to the collection of particles on my chest.

"So—" he says.

"Right." I clear my throat. "Okay, well, here's the thing. I know you want to buy my apartment—"

"Were you not happy with my offer? Because—"

"No, no, it's not that. I just want to know *why*."

"Ah?" His face bends into a question. "Is there anything else you want to know?" This could be my chance to get answers to so many things. My brain spins.

"Well, separate from that, we were looking for some evidence about the chief. . . ."

"Charlene?"

"Right. Charlene. We thought she was maybe not on the level." What am I doing here? I need to leave. I have made a grievous error. The chief and Jack Saint have been friends going way back. I think they were maybe even romantically involved at one point. What if he tells her I came in babbling conspiracy theories about her? I have no proof of anything. I scramble to fix it.

"We?" he says.

"Yeah . . . I mean no . . . I mean me." I can't drag Bella into this. And what about Jasmine? It would end her career before she even got started.

"You." He looks amused, and I'm starting to sweat.

"Yes, *I* was looking for some evidence at the hall of records, and *I* found a deed showing you had bought Miracle Lake."

His smile widens slightly, and he leans back in his chair.

"And I'm just wondering, why? Why buy Miracle Lake? Why buy Wonderland? And why my apartment?"

The level of mirth on his face is pretty intense. Like, he's not hiding that he thinks I'm a babbling idiot. I would love to disintegrate into my chair. This is very nice leather. I could melt into its fibers and be perfectly happy.

"I'm sorry," I say. "I know this is a lot."

"Oh, oh, come now, Mary," he says. "It's all right. Let's take a breath, shall we? A sip of tea." We inhale and exhale together and then take a drink. I do feel better. "Now," he says, "I admire your gumption. In fact, I admire almost everything about you. You have survived the murder of your family, witnessed the death of thousands of people including my beautiful wife, you rescued my daughter, and when the time came, you were brave enough to cut off your love's hand. You were the recipient of a prestigious internship and were instrumental in the solving of a case that should very much have been left to the adults in the situation. You are, frankly, a wonder, and I am very pleased our paths have crossed. I think you're going to do great things with your life, truly, things that will make their mark on the Scar and Monarch as a whole and that cannot be predicted from where you and I are sitting right now, Mary." One of the birds ruffles its feathers behind him, and he reaches out to stroke it before turning back to me. "I want us both to remember this moment. Let's put a pin in it, shall we? Let's *breathe* it in. You and I here in my office as the Scar disintegrates around us and the greedy monsters in power in Monarch seek to take the focus off themselves and turn it onto four innocent children."

James, Maleficent, Ursula. "Four?"

"The Queen of Hearts," he says. "Haven't you seen? The Watch has been dispatched full force to find her now. They're crawling about as we speak." He makes little spider motions with his hands. His fingers are long and kind of creepy, and I have to fight not to hug myself.

"No, I haven't had much time for the news lately."

"Well, I've had to hire the extra help you met downstairs just to keep that awful Watch away from me. Those nattering goblins lack organization and intelligence, but they think they can do as they please and have a bloated sense of entitlement." He sighs. "I digress. Let's address your question about my intentions with regard to the acquisition of Miracle Lake and your home that is adjacent to it. While I might give you some advice about the ill effects of equivocation and apologetics when making a request for information, it's to be understood given our power differential. However, Mary, I'm not ready to tell you or anyone else why I'm doing anything, nor should I have to. I've earned the right to my own timing." He slides the tray with the teapot and sugar and cream over to the side and reaches for my hand. "May I?"

I nod, not sure what's coming next. He takes my hand in his. "I want you to know that you are not alone. You have an ally in me, and I assure you that what I am doing I am doing for the Scar. And I promise you, Mary, I have some goodies up my sleeve you're going to be so pleased with. The people who have sought to destroy the Scar have no idea what's coming for them. No idea at all. Ah," he says, glancing behind me, his tone changing instantly. "You're back."

"Yes, I got extra pickles like you said," the deep voice booms. "Oh! Miss Heart! So nice to see you!"

Anton, Jack Saint's loyal giant who was also his security until recently, hovers in the doorway, taking up the entire space. He's grinning at me, holding a paper bag by two ropy straps that disappear in his hands.

"And you got one for yourself?" Jack says.

"Yes, I did. No extra pickles for me, though."

"Excellent for the digestion." Jack gets to his feet, and I stumble to mine, disoriented by subtext and new information. "But to each his own."

"I'm going to go," I say.

"All right, Anton can show you out." Jack comes around the desk and gives me another brief hug. "I have my eyes on you," he says, and takes the bag from Anton.

As I leave, I realize two things: One, I'm even more confused than I was when I walked in. And two, Jack Saint having his eyes on me could mean many things, and the possibilities fan through my imagination until I'm certain.

Jack Saint has been watching me.

SIXTEEN

THE NEXT MORNING, I HEAD TO BELLA'S BRIGHT and early. We're going to meet the man with the dagger tattoo, and I've done just what she asked and gotten myself together as professionally as possible. I've even polished my boots. But when I reach Bella's house, there are people everywhere. Maybe the press? The Watch? There are no cameras, no signs of any gray suits or white cars lining the street. It looks like . . . moms. Scar moms and a couple of dads. Or at least middle-aged, stressed-out people, which usually means a parent.

The door is cracked and Bella's mother, Fantasia, is mid-sentence: ". . . can't do it for you. I'll send you all the blessings I have, but it's not like it used to be."

She sounds distressed, and when she sees me, she holds the door open and ushers me inside. "I'm sorry," she says to the people, and closes the door.

Aunt Stella is at a distance, wringing her hands. "I don't know what to do. Should we invite them in?"

Fantasia shakes her head. "Give them false hope? We don't have magic."

They both seem to remember at the same time that I'm standing there and swoop in to hug me in a swirl of lace and satin.

"Hi!" I say from where my face is smushed into Stella's collarbone. "Bella and I were just going to take a walk over to the—"

"Dragonfly Park." Bella comes charging down the stairs, putting the backing in a silver stud earring. She mouths *Sorry* and says, "Did you see those people outside? They all came over here because this place was supposed to make dreams come true and they want their kids back. Someone started a rumor that the House of Fantasia is back in business. Heartbreaking, right?"

I peer out the window. They've gathered in a circle and are holding hands, their lips moving in what I imagine is a prayer. It must be so scary not to know where your kids are.

Stella crosses her arms and leans against the door. "No harm in letting them stay there, but I'm not ready to let them in."

"We've learned to live with it," Fantasia says, "but it's not easy reminding people that we can't grant anything anymore. They forget, anyway, that all granted wishes come at a cost."

"Weeping people at my door are the last thing I need to see in the morning while I'm trying to eat my toast," Stella grumps. "And I want every last shred of that nonsense off my wall." She points to the mind map in the great hall. "I'm out of patience. Bad enough I have to see all those people on the news spewing so much nonsense."

"I told you I will get it all down by tonight," Bella says.

"You're just going to transfer it into your room. I want all that bad energy out," Fantasia says.

"Mom!"

"I want you to be happy, that's all." Fantasia turns her attention to me and cups my cheeks in her hands. "You come back anytime you like, okay? But maybe use the back door, just until all this settles down."

"Come on," Bella says. "Let's escape while we can."

It turns out Bella was just saying she was going to Dragonfly Park so Stella and Fantasia wouldn't ask any questions. We're really headed to the Tea Party, where we find Jasmine reading a paper with the headline "Where Is the Red Queen?" and the subheading "No One Is Safe." I try to read a few lines of the Red Queen article without looking too obvious, but I can't get a good enough look.

Jasmine has on a baseball cap and sunglasses, almost easy to overlook next to a small gathering of the Defunct Fairy Godmother Society (I can tell because they're wearing DFGS T-shirts) and a bunch of starved-looking Legacy club kids sipping on coffee drinks, trying to recover from last night.

As soon as Jasmine sees us she rolls up her paper and tucks it in her bag. "Know your enemy," she says, then gives us both kisses on either side of our cheeks. "Everyone all right today?"

"Fine," Bella says. "You?"

"I saw him go in about an hour ago," Jasmine says. "He came out, got some coffee, and took it back up to his apartment."

"How do you know it's him?"

She pulls out her phone and shows me a picture of him and a close-up of his dagger tattoo. I only saw him for a minute or two in Caleb Rothco's tattoo shop and then once on the street, but I recognize him. Bella is nodding, too.

"Oh yeah, that's him," Bella says.

"Good." Jasmine pockets the phone. "He and Caleb Rothco go way back. Went to nursery school together. Both fixtures in the Scar, Legacy all the way."

"How did you find all this out?" I try hard to keep the admiration out of my voice, but it's tough.

"A journalist is only as good as her sources." She takes a last sip of coffee and puts some money on the table, weighing it down under a saucer. "I have informants just like every other reporter."

I imagine her meeting with people in dodgy alleyways, and my respect for her goes up another notch.

"Are we really going to do this?" Bella asks. "It doesn't seem safe."

"You were a cop a week ago," I remind her. "I never saw you hesitate about talking to anyone."

"I know, but I had a gun. I had a badge and the authority to question a person of interest in a criminal case. If a cop saw me here now, they'd probably arrest me for messing with an active case."

"I've got a weapon," Jasmine says, opening her bag so we can see the small teal-colored can of pepper spray attached to her keys. "And I'm a journalist and have a press pass. We'll think of something if it comes to that. Sometimes people surprise you. Sometimes they're just waiting to talk."

"I have my boots and a knife," I confess.

"Boots?"

"Steel toes. They aren't just for looking pretty. I think between the three of us we can handle him."

"I don't like to be unprepared," Bella grumbles.

But she goes up the stoop first anyway and pushes all the intercom buttons until the gate buzzes and we're in, quickly, before anyone can get to a window to look and see who might be waiting.

"It's 4-A," Jasmine says, referencing her phone again.

There's only a small entryway and no sign of an elevator or anything, just a sad plastic plant near the stairs. This is one of the Scar's oldest buildings, and it smells a little musty with the faint trail of trash. We only stop when we arrive in front of his apartment.

"Do we knock or what?" I whisper. "Should we say we're police?"

"Seriously?" Bella says. "That's a felony!"

Jasmine gives me a look. "Is this your first day? Do you know the penalty for impersonating an officer?"

I think guiltily of sneaking into the prison to talk to Caleb, stealing the officer's uniform and probably getting her into trouble.

"Hello? It's the . . ." Bella stammers.

"Jasmine Bizhan. We spoke yesterday?"

The door opens, and there's Tattoo Guy in the flesh. I didn't realize how intimidated I would be, but I am. He's tall and skinny with a hooked nose, maybe in his late twenties. Did I mention he's tall? So, so tall. He looks down at us.

"I remember you from Caleb's tattoo shop. You can come in if you want, but I have to pack."

Jasmine and I go in, Jasmine's hand in her bag, ready to pull out her pepper spray if she needs it. Bella stays by the door with her phone in one hand and a foot keeping it from closing, like a human doorstop. My knife is in my boot. I would only need half a second to retrieve it.

Our fear and preparation are all for nothing. Trent McCutcheon is much more interested in shoving what he can into a duffel bag than he is in us.

"I'm Bella Loyola—" Bella starts.

"I know who you are. You used to be a cop. So did this one." He points at me. "You both got canned trying to tell people the truth about what's been going on in this poison palace we call a home."

Bella and I glance at each other.

"Legacy Loyalty," I say.

"All right." He seems to be seeing me for the first time. "Legacy Loyalty." He raises his fist to show me his mark.

I raise mine in return.

Jasmine shows him her phone and presses play in order to record a memo. "Are you still willing to go on record about everything you witnessed?"

He checks his watch. "Yeah, but we need to hurry. Let's do it."

Jasmine takes a shuddering breath.

"I'm a street artist who's lived in the Scar my whole life," Trent says. "I come from the picture people."

Picture people had some of the best Scar magic. They could paint or draw something with chalk, and then you traveled through it and went to the place they depicted. If one of them drew a picture of a beach, you could step through and be right there.

"The chief paid me off to set up Caleb Rothco to take the fall for murdering those two girls," Trent goes on. "I've known him my whole life. He's always been a prick, but a few months ago, he started really losing it. He did that guy in the boxes, chopped him all to hell. That was some horrifying stuff, but he didn't actually kill the guy. That dude was already dead, came to a bad end after a party night and wound up in the alley behind the tattoo shop. I want that on record, too." He points to Jasmine's phone. "Make sure you get that. He had too much to drink. Too much of everything. If anyone had bothered to check his blood levels, they would have known the guy was toast long before Caleb got to him. But yeah, he decided to hack him to pieces all right, use his body to send a message to the folks uptown that the Scar was on the map and Legacy couldn't be ignored.

"He thought, Mad Hatter, sounded kind of cool and every-thing, so he picked that name and developed this whole other menacing persona. It was just him being a show-off like always.

But then, once the chief had evidence against him for that, she thought why not get him for everything. They picked me up for vandalism when really I was just making an uninvited mural, and when they had me in a holding cell, the chief approached me with a deal. She had me set him up for everything. She got rid of those graffiti charges, which by the way could have landed me with five years in the can, in exchange for information about the Mad Hatter's dastardly deeds." He snorts. "But then, once we got a little friendly, she paid me off to plant evidence to make it look like he was the one using the magic to make the villains. She was covering for Attenborough at the time—and for herself, too, since she has a stake in the company. But that alliance won't last much longer. There can be only one person with all the power. I bet she wishes she had taken Attenborough down while she could, before he became a man of the people." He says the last part with a sneer. "But she wanted to bring down her murder stats and get internal affairs off her trail, and he was the perfect patsy. She had a bunch of other cold cases she wanted pinned on him, too. So I did what I was told. All the charges against me were dropped, and I have what I need to get out of Dodge and start fresh some-where new."

He zips up the bag and hangs it over his shoulder.

"From what I could gather, the chief and Attenborough are so tied up in business with Dally Star fronting as the Legacy man for both of them that it's going to be a bitch to pull them apart. I don't think it's going to be a friendly undoing, if you know what I mean, and I'm not sticking around for it. Turns out I've had another, better invitation. And here's a hot tip: They can look for Caleb all they want, but they're not going to find him. Where he's gone, they can't go."

"How much money did the chief pay you?" Jasmine says.

Trent crooks one side of his mouth. "Pirate's booty." He lets out a loud resounding cackle. "You think this is about *money*? They never gave me money." He shakes his head. "You really have no idea what's going on, do you?"

I think he's going for the door, and then I spot a mirror on the far wall. It's long and oval with a black wood trim. As I watch, it seems to shimmer like water. Trent looks over at me. "I'd best be on my way." His eyes glow red and he grins, and the grin is just for me. He takes two long strides away from us. The surface of the mirror ripples even more.

"Where are you—" Bella has time to say before Trent runs through the mirror and disappears.

I run after him, but the surface has turned solid again, and I hit the glass with a thud.

"What the hell are you doing?" Bella asks. "What just happened?"

"I told you!" I yell. "This is magic. *Magic!*"

Jasmine presses a button on the phone and stares at the mirror. Her eyes are shining, hands shaking. "All right," she says. "Everyone. Cards on the table. What do we know?"

We all flop to the ground. I stay close to the mirror just in case something happens. I have no doubt that if it opened up or if that glass rippled, I would jump right through it after him.

"Okay," Bella says, "what do we have?"

"A shady deal between Trent and the chief. A firsthand account of the chief's corruption on your phone," Jasmine says.

"Deeds to Miracle Lake, Monarch Lab Corps, and Wonderland—all listing the chief, Dally Star, and Kyle Atten-borough as co-owners," Bella continues.

"Kyle Attenborough was somehow able to manufacture magic," Jasmine goes on.

"But Wrong Magic—"

"Right. That only works on Legacy."

"I have two more things," I say.

They both look up sharply, like they're just realizing I'm in the room.

"Well, go on!" Bella says. "Don't just sit there!"

"Yesterday I went to see Jack Saint," I say.

Bella's mouth drops open, then snaps shut. "And you didn't think this was something you needed to tell me?"

"I'm telling you now. Are you going to listen?"

"Fine," she says. "Go on."

"I was in a mirror store, Reflections. There was some weird stuff going on in there. A guy paid thousands of dollars for a mirror. I bet there's some kind of connection."

I flip over the mirror next to me, and when it's turned upside down, we can all see the gold foil sticker that says REFLECTIONS on it.

"Magic?" Bella murmurs.

"Yeah, like I was telling you yesterday. This isn't the same world we lived in a few weeks ago. We haven't ever seen this world before. We need to adjust."

"Okay, so how does this relate?"

"It relates because if the chief and Dally and Kyle owned the lake, Wonderland, and the lab until Jack started strong-arming them out of those properties, there's only one thing that makes any sense as to why that would be so important. What is at the center of all of it?" I pause and wait, and they both look at me blankly. "OMG, seriously? What is the biggest mirror in all of the Scar?"

Bella gasps and Jasmine grips her wrist. "Miracle Lake," they both say at once.

I slump back, exhausted from trying to get them to see.

"Yeah," I say. "It's so obvious, right? Miracle Lake *is* the source of magic, the vortex. Something happened with the Fall or whatever. They built the building right over the vortex, and when the building went down, some of the magic went to the surface. Kyle Attenborough and the chief must have figured that out. That's where Kyle was getting the seed of magic to mass-manufacture it."

"But it didn't work out the way they'd planned and the whole thing backfired," Jasmine says. "Except someone must have figured out how to get magic into the mirrors."

"Which people are now paying thousands of dollars for and using as portals to who knows where," Bella finishes.

"And now I'm pretty sure since Jack Saint is fighting them, they're trying to take back control with Kyle running for mayor," I say.

"There are still some pieces missing," Jasmine says. "Trent said there's tension between Attenborough and the chief. Why? And what does it mean? Before I can put all this in the paper I'm going to need to be able to see the whole picture. Quick. Let's go back to the paper! I've been working on an article and I want to get this added in."

When we get back to the *Genie's Lamp*, Bella attacks the deeds and all the paper we've collected, spreading it out on Jasmine's desk. Meanwhile, Jasmine introduces me to her boyfriend, Al, a kind-faced guy with a monkey on one shoulder. Bella waves at him, only sparing him a moment before she returns to her task.

"So I'm pretty sure this is going to make you mad, because this isn't my story, but . . ." he tells Jasmine.

"What? Spit it out!"

"Oh, my love. You are so gentle, so demure. . . ."

Jasmine rolls her eyes. "He makes me sound like an ogre, but really it's just a boundary we have to have. Work is work."

Bella looks up from the deed she has in her hand. "Did you know the chief serves on seven boards, four of which are owned by Kyle Attenborough—" Then she startles and sits upright. "I'm sorry," she says, "did you say something?"

"Still the same old Bella," Jasmine says.

"Is anyone interested in what I have here?" Al says.

"Hand it over," Jasmine says.

"First let me explain." He holds the papers out of reach, and I can tell Jasmine wants to swipe them out of his hand. "People down at the courthouse are getting more and more upset about everything that's going on. It's no secret the chief and Kyle are at odds and he's trying to distance himself from her so he can branch out, whatever that means. So this guy I've been talking to says Kyle plans to leak these documents in the next couple of days, and he's going to throw the chief under the magic carriage, smother her with the magic carpet—"

"Okay, we get it." Jasmine motions with her hands for him to hurry.

"So they're leaked to us early."

Al gives Jasmine the papers. "This is unbelievable."

Bella gets up and grabs the papers from Jasmine. She gasps. "The chief has been laundering money through Kyle Attenborough's organizations! Hundreds of thousands of dollars. She's not going to be able to prove where that money comes from. It has to be payoffs or something, or illegal activities."

"We've got her, Mary. We've got the chief red-handed. There's nothing she's going to be able to do to defend herself now. Kyle Attenborough is going to take her down."

"Not if I get there first," Jasmine says. "Al, save me the front page tomorrow. It's going to take me most of the night to get this right, but I'm going to be the one to drop this, no one else, and I'm not giving Kyle the satisfaction of doing it on his terms, making himself look so innocent."

"Okay, let's do this, team!" Al rubs his hands together, and I understand now why this kind of work is addictive, just like detective work. You're not only trying to get justice and expose the truth. You're trying to do it first and best. "We'll move the press conference to 1-B."

"But, Mary," Jasmine says, keeping a respectful distance, "I do need to ask you something, and your answer is going to make or break this exposé."

"Me?" My eyes are still trailing over the figures. The chief received campaign donations for fifteen thousand dollars, deposited them into one of Kyle's businesses, then withdrew the money in salary. She did this over and over again. It's brazen. She had to think she was so powerful no one would ever call her to account.

"Yes, you." Jasmine gently presses down on the pages so I'm forced to meet her eyes. "You're the key to everything. I need you to tell me your story, everything you saw the night of the battle, everything you love about your friends that you want the world to know. I need you to tell me the truth so I can pass it along to everyone in Monarch. We have everything we need to nail the chief, but what we need now is to help everyone understand what happened to the so-called villains—how they were kidnapped, coerced, persuaded, groomed, and betrayed by the people who are supposed to be looking out for them." She waits for all this to sink in. "Can you do that for me? For yourself?"

I look over to Bella, unsurprised by the torrent of emotion about to burst out of me. My tears have been just below the surface all day.

I don't know if I can be a spokesperson for everything my friends went through, because I'm not one of them. Not yet anyway. And I made my choice—to stay. They must think I don't care. But now maybe wherever they are, maybe they'll be able to pick up a paper and see that I'm here for them, that I miss them and still love them.

Maybe if they see that, they'll come get me out of this hellhole and take me with them where I always should have been from the beginning.

"Yes," I say. "I'll give you a full interview."

Bella claps. "Yes," she cries. "Let's do this!"

Jasmine jumps to her feet. "I can't write all of it. Some of it is speculation, but I have enough. I have enough documents and the interview. I can show corruption and collusion, and I can theorize about Miracle Lake and demand studies be done." She pulls me up into a huge hug. "Thank you both! I have to go!"

Bella and I are left staring at each other. I feel so tired, sad, and jealous that I can't be wherever Trent went. I want to escape everything.

"Hey," Bella says, "you okay?"

"Yeah. Someday everything's going to be ponies and rainbows, right?"

She pats my head and threads her arm through mine. "Oh, honey," she says, "I sure hope so."

And then the chaos starts up.

SEVENTEEN

WE RUN OUTSIDE AS THE CROWD BUILDS.

Bella points. "Look. They're going toward Miracle. Something must be going on!"

"When is something *not* going on at Miracle?"

"Apparently never," Bella murmurs.

"Come on, girls. I smell a story." Jasmine pulls on my sleeve, and we're caught in the current.

The road is so filled with people I can hardly move, a parade of animal heads and girls in rainbow wigs dancing and kicking up their feet, and as I make my way farther up the road, a marching band rolls out in front of me, playing "What's Goin' on in the Scar." Bubbles float through the air and people fling glitter at one another.

As we approach the stage, I see the signs plastered everywhere along with pictures of Kyle.

KYLE ATTENBOROUGH FOR MAYOR

ENOUGH IS ENOUGH

#VILLAINSNOMORE

#LOOKTOTHELIGHT

#ALLFORONE

#SAVETHESCAR

The expensive suits and the fur-lined coats Kyle Attenborough used to sport around town are gone. I don't even see his usual buffed-out, shiny nails. In the picture, Kyle Attenborough doesn't look like the king of the Narrows and he doesn't look like Legacy, either. He looks like no one and nothing and everyone and everything. Like one of us, but better—like the one who is going to *save* us. His eyes appear shrewd yet soft. He's been shot from below so he's kind of godlike, but he also looks somewhat . . . humble?

This is the biggest load of goblin snot I've ever seen in my life. He's a complete troll of a human being. Sticking him in a boring button-down shirt and wringing the pomade out of his hair isn't going to change that. Nothing is ever going to erase the vision of him, his blue eyes cold and unfeeling as he sent his henchmen after James and me. He didn't care about anything except making sure we didn't tell his secret. It turns out that even when it was revealed that he was experimenting on Scar children to try to make magic come back, it didn't matter. No one gave a crap.

You know what? We should kill him. Hack him into pieces. Wouldn't it be wonderful to cut him limb from limb? Off with his head?

Oh good. You're back.

Been here all along. Didn't you miss me, though?

Not at all.

You're lying.

"Well, come *on*." Bella tugs at me. "If we're going to be here, let's get to the front."

"Remind me to take you with me the next time I go to a concert," I say.

My phone buzzes. It's Gia making sure I'm okay. She would normally be sleeping right now, but I'm sure she can't rest with all the noise outside. I text her quickly to let her know I'm fine, and we push ahead.

A couple passes by riding atop a float. The man throws the woman into the air and catches her again. They laugh and hug. The crowd reaches an absolute fever pitch as we approach the podium and Kyle Attenborough takes the stage. He's in the same uniform he was wearing in the posters. He's softened, a bit rounded, weathered like a friendly cowboy.

The woman beside me screams, face streaked in tears.

Kyle makes a motion to calm everyone down. The band stops. The revelry pauses.

I would like to walk away. I haven't seen Kyle Attenborough since his goons were chasing me down, trying to shoot all of us and take us captive. I remember what he said to me just before they hauled him away (very temporarily, as it turns out). *You think you just saved the city, but you have murdered every one of its citizens.*

What about what *he* did?

"Look at this gorgeous weather, huh?" He beams and lifts his hands skyward. As he does so, the clouds part and sun shines down on us for the first time since the villains escaped.

More cheers.

"Thank you, thank you, and thank you for being here. It's a great day for the Scar and for you, and it is my great honor to be here as well, with you."

There's thunderous clapping, but it dies down quickly.

"I'd love to draw this out," he continues, "but the stakes are too high for that, so let's just get to it, because there's no time to waste. I'm here today to officially announce my candidacy for mayor of this great city."

The crowd explodes, and it's several minutes before Kyle can get it under control.

"I was never going to do this." He puts up his hands to

demonstrate his innocence. "I thought, 'Monarch has its leaders and they do a pretty good job, right?'"

Booing all around.

"But I've made some discoveries that have made it impossible for me to go on being a businessman of the people and for the people in good conscience." He throws his shoulders back, but his voice gets lower, more intimate. "This city is in peril. It's been a week since the Battle of Miracle Lake, since monsters terrorized this city and continue to do so daily. And what has been done to help? Set up the Watch? What has the Watch done? Nothing. You know why? Because they have no power." He emphasizes this with one long finger. "All they can do is creep around in fancy cars and scare our kids at school. All the hype, and you know what? They're glorified security guards. Me? If I was in charge of the Watch, I would give them more than that. Let them do the job they actually came to do, stop humiliating them. Let them take action, find out what's going on, bring the villains to justice. Because guess what, guys? Six more Legacy kids Vanished this week. Poof! And what is our mayor doing about it? What have the police accomplished? Nothing, nothing, and more nothing.

"Meanwhile, we've got another problem on our hands. A whole new villain. This Red Queen waltzed right into our jail and freed our most dangerous criminal. She's leaving messages all over town like it's a game. And I'll tell you what. I'm betting she's the one kidnapping our children. The biggest worry is that we just don't know. We don't know anything about her, and what is anyone doing to get to the bottom of it? What is Mayor Triton's plan to get Monarch back under control?"

He puts a hand behind his ear and leans forward.

"Nothing!" the crowd yells.

"And what do we think they're going to do if we don't stop them, if we don't take some action?"

"Nothing!"

"That's right. That's right. I don't think nothing is good enough. *I* expect more than that. I want to see what the Scar, what the great city of Monarch, is capable of when we put ourselves together and unite to overcome. We're going to find the villains and our children, and we're going to bring those kids home safely. Under my watch, there will not be nothing, there will be a whole lotta something. We're going to get the Red Queen, the Mad Hatter, all of them. Every. Single. One." He points to the center of his upraised palm for emphasis. "We're going to bring all of them to justice, no question. And I'll tell you something else. We're going to do it fast. Just get me in that office and I'll show them how it's done. Enough of this incompetence. Enough already!"

The crowd goes wild. People are losing it, shrieking like this guy is a rock god. And apparently he's not ready to shut up yet.

"True, true," he says, "when the Battle of Miracle Lake happened, they tried to blame me because I'm an investor in Monarch Lab Corps, but it didn't stick. I'll admit, I wanted to help bring magic back. I wanted to return the Scar to its former glory—of course I did. Who wouldn't? It's a beautiful place and deserves to be what it once was. There's no shame in that. But as soon as I saw that my efforts weren't working, I pulled out." He pauses for effect. "But the vicious villains wanted more. They got greedy. They wouldn't take no for an answer. They stole from me and cheated and lied. My son tried to stop them, but they got the vials of the Elixir before we could destroy them. Now Chief Ito and Mayor Triton and their cronies are out to get me, trying to drag my name through the mud. But I'm a businessman. I'm not afraid of Triton and I can take whatever she can dish out. All I need is your vote and your support, and I will bring the Scar through this terrible time. I promise. That's my word, and I never break my word. Are you with me, Monarch?"

The crowd flails around again, screaming about vengeance against Chief Ito and Mayor Triton for all the *unfairness*, for trying to persecute an innocent man.

I may actually vomit.

"No, no." He makes calming hand motions. "Let's be mature. I forgive them for that. I really do. Let's let bygones be bygones. But that doesn't mean we let them keep going with this terrible behavior. Listen to me. I'm talking directly to Legacy now." It's so quiet the only sounds are the cooing of pigeons and the occasional clearing throat. "Chief Ito and Mayor Triton are not your friends."

Another round of hisses starts up.

"They don't care about you. And look, I was the same at first. I was raised in the Narrows with the same stories everyone else got. The Scar was full of dirty, lazy people. Ever since the Death of Magic, Legacy are worthless. But when I bought a building and started going down there and got to know the people, I realized there's so much beauty and value in the culture and traditions of the Scar. You are all precious and deserve the attention and support of your government services. Heck, when I saw how great the Scar is, I moved my son, Lucas, down here. The Narrows is great, Midcity is great, and if we united, just imagine how powerful we could be." He waits for the crowd to hoot and holler, then calm. "And I can tell you this much: If magic ever does come back, all the way back, I want to be on the right side of history. Here, with you. I may not be Legacy, but I promise you this: To you I will be loyal."

My eyes would detach themselves from their sockets if I could roll them as far back in my head as I want to.

"If you elect me as your mayor," he says, winding down, "I promise I will represent your needs, your voices, and that I will root out the corruption in Monarch from top to bottom, starting with that crooked police chief and ending with those vile, venomous, vicious villains."

The crowd goes wild again. Ticker tape explodes everywhere. Bella and Jasmine and I all stare at each other, speechless.

"A vote for Kyle Attenborough is a vote for the Scar and for a united Monarch. Because enough is enough!" he finishes, and throws one arm into the air. "All for one!"

Everyone around me begins chanting, "ALL FOR ONE! ALL FOR ONE! ALL FOR ONE!"

"So," Jasmine says, "back to the paper? We need to finish what we started."

I'm about to say yes, when I feel a hand on my shoulder and jump, ready to reach into my boot for my knife.

"Easy," the voice says.

"Anton?" I say when I realize that the voice is attached to Jack Saint's bodyguard. I surprise myself by throwing myself into his arms, and he surprises me by patting me on the back.

"There, there," he says, then smiles at Bella. "I know you. Detective Loyola!"

"Not a detective anymore, sadly."

"For now," he says.

"This is Jasmine," I say.

"Yes. Bizhan. I'm familiar."

Jasmine shakes his hand enthusiastically.

"I'm sorry to interrupt this party, but Mr. Saint would like a word with Mary. May I steal her away?"

Bella and Jasmine both check my comfort level, and I nod. I love Anton and for some reason trust him completely. Plus, Jack Saint might finally be ready to tell me more. Whatever he has to say to me, I want to hear it.

"I'll meet you at the paper," I say to Bella and Jasmine.

"We'll get her there safely, giant's honor," Anton says.

We all hug briefly, jostled by the crowd around us, and then I follow Anton to a stretch limo that's been wedged along the sidewalk. Normally, I wouldn't get into a black town car with a couple of men, but Jack Saint and Anton are a different story. When I slip into the cool interior and take the seat across from Jack, he smiles at me and welcomes me in.

"Well, come on, Anton," Jack says. "Get in, old man."

Anton climbs in after me, his head dangerously close to the roof, and Jack taps the glass to let the driver know that we're ready to move on. We inch through the crowd.

"I didn't think I'd be seeing you again so soon, but it's certainly a pleasure," Jack says.

"Thanks?" I say.

"On your way to the *Genie's Lamp*, is it?" Jack says.

"Actually, yes." Anton hasn't had the chance to tell him anything, has he?

Jack pushes the button, and the dividing window opens. "The *Genie's Lamp*, please."

The driver nods, and it closes again.

"How did you know that?" I ask.

"I know everything."

He acknowledges my scowl.

"Nothing nefarious," he says. "Let's just say I have a stake in knowing what's going on with you. I let my daughter slip through my hands, and I'm not going to make that mistake again."

"So you're monitoring my phone?"

"Let's call it passive data collection," he says.

"Explain," I demand.

"If you mention Mally, I'm notified. I had need to find you this morning, so I may have dipped a toe in your texts." He glances at me. "And your GPS."

"Hey!" I say.

"Wouldn't you rather have me tracking you in some way so you don't get lost like my daughter?"

"This is a total invasion of privacy. And what, you won't help me, but I've been helping you without my own knowledge?"

"I beg to differ," he says, with a bow of his head. "Anton would be your greatest ally, in case of emergency."

Anton makes a noise of assent.

"And now let's talk. You've been doing very good work, Miss Heart. Very good. I happen to know there's an article underway. I came upon an incomplete draft this morning. Fascinating stuff, really."

Anton seems to be nodding off in the corner, so the atmosphere in the car feels much more personal, just Jack Saint and me.

"What do you want?" I say. "Why did you invade my personal space and then take me from the rally? You must want something."

He looks over at me. "Shrewd little thing, aren't you?"

"I don't appreciate diminutives," I counter.

He grins. "Fair enough. Sometimes you remind me of Mally, you know?"

Mally was torturing people even before she technically became a villain. Am I really like that?

You are, She says. *You know you are. You always have been.*

"But you aren't wrong," he goes on. "I do have ulterior motives for retrieving you at this particular time."

"You don't say."

"Kyle Attenborough is getting to be quite a problem. You and I both know he's behind my daughter's disappearance and that he doesn't care about the Scar at all. He wants to milk it for everything it's worth—its real estate, its labor force—and he knows exactly what Miracle Lake can do."

"Right?" I say. "That's what I've been saying, and no one will listen to me."

"The piece of article I read . . ."

"Yes?"

"It was astute and comprehensive, but somewhat lacking in important details about Kyle's part in the kidnapping of James, Maleficent, and Ursula. He's blaming everything on the chief, now that he's trying to distance himself from her, but that isn't fair, is it? He was the one. So I'll ask you to tell Miss Jasmine Bizhan in that persuasive, charming way you have that she still has some work to do before she can go to print."

"She's working on it, but she can't print those things about Attenborough because she doesn't have proof."

"Ah yes," he says. "I thought that might be a problem. So I've brought you some."

"How—"

"Now here's where it's going to get real," he says. "And I mean really, really real. I'm going to give you what you need, footage of Kyle Attenborough forcibly injecting James, Maleficent, and Ursula with the false magic. I was able to retrieve it from the Monarch Lab Corps cameras before Kyle could destroy it. I want you to take it to Miss Bizhan and ask her to incorporate it into her story. It is proof enough."

"Must be nice to have so much power," I say.

"Yes. It really is." He smirks at me. "Care for some water? We have regular and bubbly."

"No!"

"All right, then I'm going to offer to give you something else. Are you ready?"

"I guess."

"There's no guessing."

"Is it a gift?"

"A gift you have to choose to receive."

"You know, no offense, but it's already been a long day, so can you just do whatever you're going to do? I'm not in the mood for riddles and puzzles."

"As you wish." He pulls out his phone. It takes me a second to realize what he's showing me: the familiar, grainy footage of the night the Mad Hatter escaped from the prison.

"I've seen this."

"Have you?" This time instead of the Red Queen creeping out of the jail cell, I see myself. I come out, and as I cross the threshold from the door into the hallway, my clothes change from the cop uniform I had on to the red leather jacket and boots I saw in the footage on the news. My hair lengthens and curls. My movements change, too. I slide through the hall, the Mad Hatter close behind, grinning madly. We practically high-five. My face is clearly visible. It is definitely me.

It's not like I didn't know I was the Red Queen, but I thought of her as something separate. Now I see we're two sides of the same coin. It's really true. I'm a villain.

Aren't you the luckiest.

"I was able to fix the footage that the news channels received," Jack goes on. "What they showed on TV was doctored. This is the real deal. No one has it but me."

"But how? Who would doctor news footage to protect me?"

He shrugs, smiling. "All things will be revealed in good time."

I suddenly understand. "You're talking to the villains. You know where they are. You know—"

"Everything. That's right. Now will you let me finish?"

I sit back, throat dry, the world swimming before me.

"Yes."

"Since you seem to have figured it out, yes, I've talked to my Mally. She says you haven't fully integrated her. The Red Queen is you, but you have stuffed her way, way down inside. You think you can beat her, but that's impossible. You're only making it harder, delaying the inevitable. Give yourself permission to be everything you are, and become your whole self. Work with her, not against her, and you'll have power and magic beyond your wildest dreams. There's no going back, you see. There is only going forward, accepting what already is. Then, and only then, will you be able to see all of your friends again. Only then will you be able to fully understand."

I think of Gia, my mother, my sister. All the women in my life who never had any power, each a victim in her own way. If what Jack Saint is saying is true, this is my chance to change all that, not only for me, but for my family, for the Scar. And . . .

"The instant you embrace the Red Queen, you will be permitted to cross to where they are, understand?"

"What does that mean? I have been embracing her. I've been trying."

"I'm sure. Now try harder. Consider this your invitation. You know how to do it. You only need to be sure."

This is it. The invitation I've been waiting for. I don't know whether to scream or cry or hug him in relief.

Jack Saint pats my hand. "You come from the heart, Mary, and I very much admire that about you. When you fully accept who you are, that will continue to be true. That part of you will never be lost. Be bold. Let your heart lead you. It's a strength, not a weakness. You already know the truth of your destiny. Now you need to leap." He hands me a flash drive. "Give this to Miss Bizhan with my compliments to her journalistic savoir faire, and tell her to hurry with that story. I'll expect to see it printed in the news first thing tomorrow. And tell her I think she'll find it will be a whole new world for her and the *Genie's Lamp*. No more embarrassing gossip for them."

"Okay," I say, clutching the drive.

"Looks like we've arrived in spite of the traffic," Jack says. "What good luck."

Here the streets are more or less clear. Just the usual stragglers and people hanging out and chatting.

"Anton, let the young lady out of the car."

"Sir," Anton says, waking himself up. "Right, right. Of course, sir." He opens the door and waits for me to clamber out.

"Oh," Jack Saint says, "before you go, have one of these."

He slips something small into my hand. It's a button that reads JACK SAINT FOR MAYOR.

"Are you serious?" I palm it. It would take a miracle for a Legacy to get voted mayor of Monarch, especially a Legacy like Jack Saint. He's so . . . *magicky*.

"Like I said"—he adjusts his shirt and winks at me—"Kyle Attenborough will never have that job."

EIGHTEEN

"THIS IS REALLY HAPPENING?" JASMINE IS ON FIRE, pacing back and forth in front of me, the flash drive in her hand. "I'm not dreaming it?" She yanks me by the elbow into one of the smaller conference rooms off to the side and slams the door behind us, Bella sneaking in just in time. "But why would he give this to me?"

I pull my arm away.

Bella is typing things into her phone from the side, eyeing us anxiously.

"Because he wants the truth out there?"

"Oh, I think it's a little more self-serving than that," Bella says.

Jasmine nods in agreement.

"If you want to look a unicorn in the mouth, that's your problem. Take it or leave it. I have to go." I tap the flash drive. "You can tell the whole story. You can put this on your website. The scoop will be yours and all the glory that goes along with it."

Bella and Jasmine watch me for a long, quiet moment. I don't have time for this, and my nerves are trilling. I need to go home and say goodbye to Gia. I don't want to be standing here anymore while they look so suspiciously on the gift Jack Saint handed them.

They're being so goody-goody it's nauseating. This is real life. There's no absolute line between good and evil or right and wrong. Things have to get done how they have to get done, otherwise nothing ever happens.

Bella takes a step toward me. "Mary," she says carefully while Jasmine turns the flash drive over and over in her hand, "I know you want to crack this open, get vengeance on the chief, and expose what happened to your friends, but it's not just a one-way street."

"Speak English, Bella."

"The corruption from the chief, from Kyle . . . It doesn't excuse Jack Saint's or even the villains'. You can see that, can't you? Jack is doing illegal things. I know you like him, but—"

"He's trying to help. He's trying to save us."

"But," Bella insists, "it doesn't mean he can just do whatever he wants, that he's above the law. Jack's only on one side: his own. He's just using us, can't you see that?"

I roll my eyes. I can't help it. We're in an unprecedented moment, and she's acting like it's a regular Tuesday. I cross my arms in front of my chest.

"Your friends? They may not have wanted to be what they are, but they have to take responsibility for it now. They're kidnapping people, *kids*. Who knows what they're doing with them."

"If they're doing it, they have their reasons," I say. "Don't you get it? The law isn't working for us. Abiding by unrealistic ethics isn't working, either."

They don't react, just keep watching me like I'm some new creature they've never seen before.

"You can stay here all night trying to figure out wrong from right, okay, but I've got things to do."

"Be careful, Mary," Bella says.

"We're here for you," Jasmine confirms.

I pull back and find myself smiling.

I am so sick of rules and trying to win a fight I have no chance of winning. I want my own power and my own abilities, and I want them now. I never ever want to feel weak again. I want to feel like *her.*

"Thanks so much," I drawl. "I think I'll be okay. It's the two of you who need to make sure you're thinking clearly. I sure do hope you expose Kyle Attenborough and show the world what he did to my friends. I very much encourage you to make that decision."

The earnestness drops away from Bella's face. Inside, I think, *Okay, Red Queen. Let's be together now. No more separation. You and me against the world. Let's do it.* Strength coils through me.

"Mary?" Bella says. She looks terrified, and I don't hate it.

I put up a hand. "No, no. No more of you talking to me, lecturing me. It's my turn, because I have something to teach *you* for a change. You're all in your head. Thinking, thinking, thinking. If you would let yourself feel for a second, you would know what's really going on around here and what it's going to take to stop it." I glance at Jasmine. "And *you're welcome* for the amazing career and accolades you'll get along with telling the truth."

"Mary—"

The door bursts open, and one of the reporters shouts: "You have to see this!"

"We're busy," Jasmine snaps.

"Jack Saint just announced he's running for mayor."

Bella turns to me and demands, "Did you know about this?"

I pull out the JACK SAINT FOR MAYOR button, pin it to Bella's shirt, and give her a kiss on the cheek. "See you both later. Good luck battling your conscience."

When I step out onto the street, I feel good. Really good. It's such a beautiful day, and I finally let everything I was thinking out into the open. After weeks of wondering who I am and where I belong and what I'm going to do next, I finally know the answers.

The *Sea Devil* is back at Miracle, so I have to walk ten blocks, but I don't mind at all. In fact, I'm enjoying the fresh air and the time alone when an ambulance, fire truck, and two police cars wedge their way through traffic, beeping to nudge cars trapped in gridlock.

Something is happening.

It feels as though I'm outside my own body, watching myself from far away as I follow the emergency vehicles. They're moving so slowly it's not hard to keep up. The closer I get the more my wrist heats up, the more my stomach twists and my vision blurs.

When they finally stop, the police jump out and start putting up a barricade. I can't see much except that everyone's moving with urgency. It takes me another minute to get close enough to see the accident, and when I do, every hair on my head stands on end.

A gold SUV is twisted, barely recognizable. Part of it is up on the sidewalk, smashed into the side of a building. The driver-side door is caved in so badly it looks flattened into two dimensions. A woman is sitting on the sidewalk crying hysterically while a police officer with a digital pad hovers above her.

Off to the side, the EMTs have worked fast to cover a body. Someone died. I hear one of the EMTs say the name *Attenborough*. I rub my thumb into my Seed mark, which is aching now, and bolt toward them.

"Hey!" I yell.

"Don't cross that line," a beat cop tells me.

"Did you say Attenborough?"

"None of your business."

"I just want to know what happened. Which Attenborough?"

The guy scowls at me.

They're wheeling a gurney, a white sheet over it, toward the ambulance. An expensive shoe flops out to the side, and I take a breath. It's not Lucas. He was in sneakers the last couple times I saw him. But that means—

"This is the big guy," he says, waving a car toward an alternate route. "Kyle Attenborough."

"He's dead?" I say.

The cop grimaces. "He's not heading home for milk and cookies."

People are beginning to gather. A woman who overheard my conversation with the cop sinks to her knees and lets out a long and painful wail. As the news begins to spread through the crowd, the sounds of mourning start up, catching like a brushfire. It won't be long before Kyle Attenborough supporters are throwing themselves in the street, their last and best hope dashed, and I'm sure it will only take hours for all of Monarch to find itself in mourning. But I have two things running through my mind. One, who did this? And two, Lucas. I'm surprised to find him in my thoughts, little cancerous infiltrator that he is, but I can't help it, and for the first time, I don't see him as some awful perpetrator. His dad said he "let" him live in the Scar, but Lucas said he was sent here because he and his dad were on the outs. And now he's lost his dad for good. He's an overprivileged kid who's basically alone in the world, not even surrounded by the usual sycophants anymore.

And then there's Jack. He said Kyle would never have the job of mayor, and now he won't. I wonder if Jack would go this far. To save the Scar from Kyle Attenborough, maybe it's worth it.

Feels good to see the truth for what it is, doesn't it?

Yes, but also, Lucas is about to find out his father is dead.

I leave the crowd behind. Things are going to get ugly, fast.

* * *

When I get home, Gia is on the couch asleep, a still photo of Kyle Attenborough and the car accident on the TV. Her eyelids flutter open, but she's fighting to keep them that way.

"Mary, you're okay. Thank all the wizards. I haven't been able to sleep all day." She yawns and rubs at her eyes.

The apartment feels eerie, simultaneously familiar and entirely unknown, like so much has happened since the last time I was here that I don't even recognize it anymore. That couch we've always had looks small and misshapen, everything in the room contorted.

"You're okay?" she says, trying to get to her feet.

I help her. "G, you should go to bed."

"I know. I wanted to see you come home safe. I wanted to make sure you were in one piece. I was so nervous, and it seems like every five minutes there was some new announcement on the news. Kyle Attenborough running for mayor, then Jack Saint, and now Attenborough is dead?" She clutches my arm, struggles against sleep. "That can't have been an accident, can it?"

"Don't worry about that now, G. Time for bed. We can talk about it when we see each other again." I can't bring myself to tell her I'll see her when she gets up tonight, because that would be a lie.

I won't be here. And if all goes according to plan, I won't be coming back until everything is resolved.

"Come on." I help her down the hall, into her room. I don't come in here much, mostly because it's a shrine to my mom, Mira, and my grandparents, who never recovered from the murders and died not long after them. I leave the lights off, imagine them watching me from the shadows. If I saw them now, had to look at their pictures, I don't know if I'd be able to do what I plan to do next.

We're late, we're late, for a very important date.

"Auntie G?" I sit down next to her.

She's already mostly asleep again. She'll probably think this was all a dream when she wakes up, and maybe that's for the best.

"Mmm?" she says.

"I just wanted to tell you how much I appreciate everything you've done for me. You've been a really, really good mom."

"Thank you."

I rest my cheek on her hand. "I'm going to be okay, better than okay. I'm going to save the Scar."

"Yes, you are, honey." She smiles, eyes still closed. "You can do anything you want."

I kiss her cheek and try to freeze her so I can remember her like this until the next time we see each other. I don't know when that will be, and I know she'll worry while I'm gone, but it will be worth the wait in the end.

I turn on the fan for her, then slip through the door to my room and run to my magic mirror. Gia has hung it up for me so it's the first thing I see when I enter. Everything hinges on this mirror and what it can do, or what I can do with it, and right now it looks so ordinary. Ordinary like me.

I walk over to it, then rub at my Seed mark. The heart on my wrist heats under my touch and then sizzles like it's electric. It hurts, but it isn't an unpleasant hurting. It's the kind that reminds you you're alive.

"Magic mirror on the wall," I say. "Show me a picture of them all."

The glass immediately wavers. My reflection ripples. Shadows emerge slowly from the silver, taking shape before me. James, long and thin; Ursula, round and full as a peach; Maleficent and the horns she grew in the lab.

The quiver ceases, the glass flattens, and the mirror goes back to normal.

CITY OF HOOKS AND SCARS

There's someone at my window.

I fling back the curtains, and there is freaking Lucas Attenborough.

"What the hell are you doing here?" I'm ready for a fight, but as soon as he comes into the room, his swollen face stops me from doing or saying anything. I just feel sad for him.

"I have something for you," he says. "You're going to want it." He saunters around the room, staring at the corkboard where I've posted all the pics of Ursula and James and me. He pauses at my picture of James and me hugging and kissing in a blatant selfie inside the Ever Garden, magical plants all around us. I know how we look: utterly in love.

All Lucas would have to do is check out my social media and he would see the same pics, but he peers at them intensely anyway, then looking around the room again, he says, "You're neater than I thought you'd be." Then something in his face changes as though he's made a decision, and he pivots a quarter turn in my direction. "I think he actually had a change of heart about the Scar."

"Your dad?"

"Yeah. We'd just started talking again. Today, right after the rally, he called me, and we met at Wonderland. He gave me this." Lucas pulls two vials from his pocket. The liquid inside is golden and frothy.

"The magic?"

"No," he says. "It's an antidote."

An antidote. I remember wanting this so badly. But I've moved on since then. The time for antidotes has passed.

"And what about the other one?" I ask, pointing to the second vial in Lucas's hand.

"I'm going to keep it. Just in case we need to make more. I

mean, if I can figure out how to make it without my dad. He was just explaining everything to me when he got a call and rushed out, and then . . ." His voice wobbles, and he takes a second to recover.

"I'm sorry, Lucas." And in that moment, I really am. Even though I hate his family and everything that they stand for, I sort of get that none of it was his fault.

"Yeah," he says.

I hold the warm glass vial, rolling it in my palm. "And how do I know it's not poison or something?"

He shrugs. "You don't. But I really, really think he was trying to do the right thing."

"What about all that stuff he said at the announcement today? About getting the villains and all that."

Lucas smiles a little and zips his hoodie to the top. "I didn't say he wasn't still a politician. Being tough on crime is good for campaigns."

"Yeah."

"I guess I'd better get going," Lucas says, peering out the window. "Looks like the news van moved on."

"You take care, Lucas." I mean to be casual, maybe even a little sarcastic, but the words come out with more feeling than I thought they would. I know what it's like to lose family. I know how much it stings.

He pauses and looks at me searchingly. "You know," he says, "I treated you like a total sack of crap in school, but I always admired you. You weren't all blustery and superior like your friends."

"Superior? Narrows kids are the superior ones."

"Us? Nah. We just have money. You all have the whole history of magic and all the potential for more, and you wear it like crowns, like the whole world should worship you. Legacy kids treat everyone else like they're missing something." He nods at my Seed mark. "Doesn't feel great to the rest of us. I think that's why my dad was trying to capture it, you know? Level the playing field a little."

"But . . . we have nothing."

"You have *everything*. You have the Legacy Seed; you have a free spirit; you have possibility."

I'm stunned into total silence. I have never thought about any of this the way he's talking about it. I can kind of see how he could think all of us in the Scar were jerks, how it could be aggravating to have so many classes about magic, how annoying it must be to have all the school clubs be about magic.

"Lucas—"

"Eh. Don't," he says. "Truth is, I kind of always thought you were beautiful, smart, and more of a person than the rest of them—a little bit of a treasure. I think that's why I was always picking fights with James, messing with your crew. I couldn't stand it that he had you and all I had was better shoes and a spot on the dais at Wonderland. All those nights I spent watching you follow James around while he and his hooligans stirred up trouble and ripped off Narrows kids . . . You're too good for him. You always were."

I step toward him as he backs out my window, but then realize I'm still in a towel.

"Bye, Mary. See you on the other side."

The other side?

And then he's gone, and towel or no towel I'm rushing to the window after him to ask him what he means by seeing me on the other side, and exactly what he knows, when my wrist starts to burn and I look down to find my Seed mark has gone from a black heart to a red one. Flames char its edges. I stifle a cry and stumble forward, crawl to my closet and force myself into clothes, all the while burning.

The glass in the mirror has gone misty and strange like it did before. It lengthens down the wall. As the shadows take shape, an earthquake starts up in me. James stares at me, hand extended, arms an ocean of muscles, jaw tensed. The other two are coming into focus as well.

My phone buzzes from the bedside table. It's Bella.

Mary. I figured something out about Miracle Lake.
The water feeds our Seed markings. You
have to use gold.

A movie pops up. Jasmine and Bella are at Miracle Lake. Jasmine has a golden spoon. The gold dips into Miracle Lake and doesn't disintegrate or anything. She taps Bella's Seed mark, and they both gasp as it turns blue and shiny. The camera pans to Bella.

"It worked!" she says excitedly. "It was on the flash drive. Kyle and one of his lab technicians were talking about it during one of the experiments. The technician thought a combination of the water and gold might be the way to make the Elixir work, but Attenborough wouldn't listen."

I was right. I was right about Miracle being the source of magic. But magic doesn't need to be injected into veins, it needs to be placed directly on the Seed.

The glass in the mirror is changing, going back to a clear reflection of the room, so I can see myself standing there holding my phone, dumbstruck. My wrist burns and pulses wildly, but the feeling that the pain is going to kill me is gone.

My phone buzzes again. I don't know where to look.

There's more. It's about the chief. We have to stop her.

It buzzes and buzzes and buzzes.

My heart picks up speed and my head spins. I might pass out. I really might.

I need you, I think. *Don't be a part of me. Let's be one and the same.*

Are you sure? the Red Queen says. *You have to be sure.*

Yes.

I feel no hesitation. I want us to be together. I want to find out what we can do.

I look in the mirror.

It's her. Or me.

Finally.

My hair is the color of cherries, and it dances out around my shoulders and wisps down my back. My lips are plumper and bright red. I feel none of the dread I'd felt when I'd seen her before. There's nothing but relief. I know who she is. I know who I am.

Everything calms down.

My heartbeat.

My Seed mark.

My fear.

Everything.

She's been me all along, calling to me, writing on walls, saving me, doing the right thing when I wasn't brave enough, telling the truth, following her heart, and breaking glass when she's not heard.

Before, I made her go away. I was afraid of her when she pulled me through the mirror, and why? What did she do? What did she ever do wrong? She helped me find my friends. She led me to them. She knew all along what I can only face now. There's something more for me in the world. There's *magic*.

I take a few steps forward and drop my phone to the floor.

I'll be back, I think.

I put my finger out and touch the glass. This time it gives and my finger goes through. This time I don't pass out. I don't fall to the floor or scream and brandish knives. I feel *good*.

The girl in the mirror extends her hand. And this time, I take it.

NINETEEN

IT DOESN'T HURT. I'M NOT SPLITTING APART. I'M coming back together. Like when I went through the mirror the night of the Battle of Miracle Lake, I'm somewhere else, a room with plush carpeting, a table with maps laid across it, bookshelves stuffed with colorful leather spines. Scar-style tea is laid out on the table, complete with silver and porcelain, tiny squares of sugar, delicate pastries.

Mally sits at the table with her crow, Hellion, perched on her shoulder; she is dressed in a black corset over a black lace top and skin-tight black pants to match. She takes a sip.

"Took you long enough," she drawls.

The floor doesn't feel stable. I try to hold my ground.

"James got all grumpy waiting for you to figure it out, embrace yourself or whatever, but now the band's back together, so yay and stuff."

"Timing is everything," James says as he comes into the room.

My knees want to give out. If Mally weren't here, I don't know what I would do. Scream and cry? Throw myself at him? Punch him in the face? One thing's for sure, though: Even missing a hand and brandishing a shiny new hook, James looks good. He's long and thinned out, black pants and a shirt slung over his body. He looks more relaxed than he did in the Scar, tanned and assured, but his eyes are still on fire like they were the night of the battle. He comes right over and hugs me.

I guess this means we don't have to have an awkward conversation about the fact that I hacked off his hand?

I want to fight him, apologize to him, kiss him, but instead I rest my head against his heart and listen to it beat for a few seconds.

"I'm so glad you're here," he says, dipping down to whisper into my ear.

"Babycakes!" Urs careens into the room and rips me out of James's arms. I laugh, because what else is there to do, and squeeze her hard. Her dress, which seems actually to be alive, wraps me up in extra tentaclelike limbs. "Love the look!"

"Yeah?" When I look down, I'm dressed in a red leather jacket with a high, wide collar that fans out around me, leather pants, and tall red boots up to my knees. My red hair reaches my waist.

"Yeah. Bold!"

"Look," a voice says from behind me. "It's my guardian angel!"

"Caleb?"

"The Mad Hatter, if you please," he says with a bow. He has meat cleavers in holsters at his side, and he catches my glance and grins at me. "What can I say? I've embraced my reputation. Welcome, dear."

"Thank you."

"Come on," James says, "let's have some tea."

"Tea," Caleb says. "That's proper."

I have so many questions I can't even think straight. We all sit down and Hellion squawks at me.

"I saw all your cousins at your apartment the other day," I tell him.

He doesn't look impressed.

I reach for the teapot and Mally snorts. "OMG, don't," she says, and points her magical staff at the pot. "So embarrassing."

"Don't be a hag," Ursula says. "She'll learn."

The teapot levitates, as do the cups. The tea pours itself and then the cups land in front of each of us.

"Cream?" Mally asks. "Sugar?"

"Both." I used to take everything undiluted, but now I want the sugar on my tongue, I crave all the sweetness.

Under the table, James takes my hand in his good one.

"Why don't you let Mary do it?" James says.

Mally looks over at us and shrugs.

"Go ahead. You do the cream and sugar," James says.

"I can't."

Yes, you can.

"Yes, you can," James says. "Everything is magic here."

I look at the cream and concentrate. "Move," I say timidly.

"That's not going to work," Urs says. "You have to really *mean* it."

"Move!" I say more forcefully. The pitcher of cream immediately sprouts legs and dashes across the table. It pours itself into my cup, then runs around the table, hastily responding to the drinkers (yes for Urs, no for the rest). When it's done, the legs disappear and it goes back to being inanimate.

"Interesting," the Mad Hatter says. "Curiouser and curiouser."

"Whatever." Mally takes a sip. "We're literally in the center of magic. It's not that impressive."

"In?" I say as Ursula flicks her wrist and magics some sweet cakes onto the center of the table.

"Well," the Mad Hatter says, "in a manner of speaking."

"We're on the other side of the mirror," Urs says, slipping a pink tea cake into her mouth.

"The flip side," James says.

"We're *in* Miracle Lake?" As it dawns on me, I understand why I saw them in the lake. It couldn't have been them exactly, of course, but the lake was giving me a hint or something, trying to make me understand, drag me through. "We're on a boat."

"A *ship*," James corrects.

"We've been here the whole time," Urs says, slapping her hands together. "Isn't it great? They're too scared to look here, and anyway, there's a whole process. The mirrors are the easiest way."

"Reflections," I say.

"Yeah, that's the place," Urs says.

I just want to be here, with them, and drink some tea, here in this place where there's still magic and I can be free, but I know it's not that easy. Nothing ever is.

"So what have you been doing here this whole time?" I ask. "I'd love to hang out all day, but I have a feeling I didn't get an invitation for nothing and you aren't hanging out here on a beach vacation."

"Astute," Caleb says.

"I think it's time," James says.

"She's going to freak," Ursula says.

"Rip the Band-Aid off," Mally says.

Hellion squawks.

"What?" I ask.

Mally taps her staff on the floor and smiles malignantly as blue light rises from it in a puff. The light builds and builds until it takes shape. Even as it does I know what's coming. The deerlike silhouette, the white stilettos that form before anything else. A few seconds later, Chief Ito is standing in front of me. She looks exactly like herself—same impeccable suit, same expensive shoes. The only difference between Chief Ito in the Scar and Chief Ito here is that here she wears a small gold crown. She takes the empty seat at the table.

I stare. It's all I can do.

"Hi, Mary," she says. "I'm sorry to have kept you in the dark for so long, to have hurt you in the way I have."

I'm so in shock I can't even speak.

"It's all been to protect you." She shakes her head. "I wanted you to have the opportunity to find your way, to let the real you out. You weren't like the others, wanting this from the beginning. You were so obsessed with being *good*. I wanted to help you. I did everything I could to guide you." She reaches across the table and puts a hand over mine. I snatch mine away. She looks at me sadly and nods. "I understand. It will take you time to forgive me."

"You . . . you . . ."

"I was doing what I had to do to keep up appearances. You have no idea how bad it is, what the people in city hall have planned for the Scar. They know magic is coming back. They know there's nothing anyone can do about it. They're going to turn the Scar into a police state. Legacy will have no freedom, do you understand?"

I'm trying to catch up.

Work, brain, work.

Can I magic myself into higher intelligence?

"I know it's a lot to take in, but I'm doing everything I can on my end. I've got people helping me—"

"Dally Star—" I mumble.

"Very good," she says.

"Jack Saint?"

"On a good day," she says, and I don't miss Mally's grimace. "I had to get Kyle out of the way, which meant an alliance of sorts." She glances at her watch. "Which reminds me: I can't stay." She looks around the table. "Thanks for letting me know Mary had arrived. I have a meeting in five minutes. Mona will be getting nervous if I don't come back. You get acclimated," she says to me. "We'll have a chance to speak soon. The others will catch you up on the plan." She blinks and is gone in a flash.

I wonder if I'll ever be able to do that.

The Mad Hatter chews on a piece of cake and keeps drinking his tea. James squeezes my hand.

"You okay, honeybee?" Urs asks finally.

"Yes, I think so." Am I? I don't even know anymore. First the chief was my hero, then my biggest disappointment, and now I don't know what to think of her. I know I like the magic, I know I like the power, I know I want to be free.

And after all this time, all the nights I stayed up hoping, wishing there were still fairy godmothers to make dreams come true, mine has. Ever since I was a little girl, I wanted the chief to choose me. I wanted to be special to her, to be just like her. Now maybe I can be. Maybe I can be as powerful, as commanding, as self-assured, and just as magical.

Maybe dreams do come true.

"So what's the plan?" I lean forward.

James grins. "That's my girl."

"Can I tell her, can I tell her?" Urs asks.

"Go ahead," Mally says.

Urs takes a deep breath, opens her arms wide, and says, "We're building an army!"

My expression doesn't change.

"A rebellion!" she clarifies. "A naughty, naughty Legacy rebellion, and we are going to smash city hall into smithereens, take over, make everything magical again, and it will all be wonderful!"

I let her words sink in for a second. The Vanished. All those kids that have gone missing; the villains have been building an army of Legacy kids.

"We have a plan, don't worry," James says.

"I'm not worried," I say. "Not when we have this." There's a charge at my fingertips. They sizzle as blue light crackles.

But what about Bella and what she discovered? What happens when everyone has it?

"Enough tea," James says. "Enough talking."

"Thank all the fairies," Mally says.

"I'm going for a swim." Urs gives me a big hug. "But we're going to catch up later. I'm talking me and you, secrets, fun, and maybe even songs. For now I'll leave you with your hunk." She swishes off, her tentacles undulating beneath her, propelling her away.

"Meeting adjourned." James stands and offers me his arm. "Come on."

He leads me up the stairs and out onto the prow of the ship, with its shiny boards. Even though he told me below that we were on a ship and I could see and feel that we were, nothing prepared me for this: a boat in the middle of a clear ocean, surrounded by a smooth sheet of water, the sun overhead, and the clockwork of industrious effort.

I suck in my breath, and James smiles widely. "Impressive, isn't it?"

Impressive isn't the word I would use, though there is certainly that.

It's *terrifying*.

All around us are giant ships, ten of them at least, bobbing in the water, #LegacyLoyalty flags on each, white with black hearts, flapping in the quiet breeze.

All James's boys are here. Damien Salt waves at me from the next ship over. They're all busy with purpose, directing magical mops and buckets of water, climbing up sails, using wands to tie knots, chatting with one another, but when they see me, they stop and stare, expressions unreadable. Behind them I recognize boys whose pictures I've seen in the papers, and I think I spy Trent McCutcheon two ships over.

Smee comes up on deck with Barnacle close behind. The dog lets me scratch him behind the ears and then sits at James's heels.

"Heck yeah, Mary! About time!" Smee comes over and claps me on the back. "We've been waiting for you to come to your senses. Cap said you would, and here you are."

"Hey, Smee."

"You with us for good, M?"

James watches me carefully.

"Yeah," I say. "I think I am."

"Great!" Smee says. "Just excellent!" He bounds away, back to work.

"I have so much to show you." James squeezes my hand.

He guides me to the edge of the boat. "Look."

Below us, Ursula floats on her back, her tentacles flipping and flopping all around her. At first, I think she's on a bed of seaweed, but then I see the writhing things all around her are eels, but not the usual faceless ones. These are long and curl around her, and they have human eyes.

"Are those *people*?" I say, as much in awe as anything else.

Ursula looks the happiest I've ever seen her, floating on her back like that, facing the sun, spinning on her own legs as the eel creatures seem to orbit around her like they are moons and she has her own gravitational pull.

"Loyalty is all," James says from behind me. He sweeps my hair from my shoulders and leans into my neck. "They didn't have any, and now they're paying the price."

I shiver. He sounds like the pirate he was always meant to be.

Behind him, the sun is setting, a bloodred orb. Gia will be waking up soon, discovering I'm not there. She'll be upset and scared. I shake off the guilt. There's nothing I can do now. I'll make it up to her later.

James cups my cheek, draws me into him, then pulls back and looks at me. "I'm the captain," he says. "Not so bad for a hooligan from the Scar, right?" I kiss his rough cheek. "I have so much to tell you."

"Yeah, I know," he says, a storm brewing over his features. "I have a lot to tell you, too. I know what's happening in the Scar with the Watch, and I know we're running out of time to save it."

"The chief—"

"There have been developments." Mally's voice cuts across the sea air. Even though she's not in her dragon form, she still has a reptilian quality to her. "Developments that can't wait for your lust. Ito's back, and she needs to see us downstairs."

Ursula is already sitting at the giant mahogany table, her tentacled dress lifeless now. A huge bowl of fruit has appeared, along with fresh bread and cheeses, and more piping-hot tea steams from the pot in the center of the table. The Mad Hatter has his feet kicked up on the table and is watching me a little too closely for my liking; Hellion has settled back on Mally's shoulder, and he ruffles his feathers and makes a few chirpy noises at me while Mally stares straight ahead. James is beside me.

None of this can be real. The seagulls squawking outside cannot be real. I'm not sure I know any of these people anymore.

Ito glides in, and this time I really have a chance to look at her. Her tailored white suit has a glowing aura.

Exactly when did the Monarch chief of police become magical?

Why did she do this? Was she always secretly on the side of the Scar? I remember her hand in mine as we stood before all those people at the press conference after my family was killed, how safe she made me feel. Maybe she *is* actually that person. Even as I think it, I know it isn't true. At least not completely. Somewhere along the line, the chief became someone else. Some*thing* else.

Caleb slides a cup of tea in her direction, and she looks at it but doesn't touch it.

"We have a problem," she says.

"Obvi," Mally says, and Ito gives her a severe look.

Caleb furrows his brows and leans in to the chief. "You actually look worried, boss. What's going on?"

"Worried is a bit of an overstatement." She folds her hands in front of her. "Let's just say I'm watching closely, and this is worth having a discussion about."

Ursula pops a piece of cheese into her mouth. "Okay, I'll bite," she says with a wink. "What's the deal, Chiefypoo?"

"Bella Loyola," Ito says. "She's the problem."

"Bella what? My Bella?" I sputter.

"You don't have a Bella," she snaps. "Not anymore. Not if you're one of us."

There's a question in the statement, and I hear it loud and clear. I look around the table, and everyone is looking at me with the same question in their eyes. Have I finally made my decision? Am I clear about who and where I want to be? Or am I maybe a traitor in their midst gathering information to use against them. Even James looks like he could use some reassurance.

"Sorry. Old habit. Bella Loyola, no more, no less."

Ito takes a moment to collect herself and says, "Bella has figured it out."

"What? How to tie her shoelaces? Ugh." Ursula leans all the

way back in her chair and looks at Ito as though she's sleepy, bored. "That girl bugs the heck out of me."

Mally cracks a smile, and James straightens beside me.

Ito holds out her hand to Ursula, and a ball of light forms in her palm. I know that light, or a version of it anyway. It's what James had, what he gave me before this all started. It's what made me what I am. From within the light something starts to form. Ursula doesn't betray anything with her expression, but I can read the nerves behind her calm. She's afraid of the chief.

The light disappears, and in the chief's palm lies an apple, bright red and shiny. She holds it out to Ursula. "Apple, my dear?"

Ursula blanches.

"You know what they say. An apple a day keeps the doctor away," the chief says. "Why don't you take one tiny bite, dear?"

"No thanks," Ursula says. "Probably poisoned it or whatever."

The chief places the apple in the center of the table. "Look at it and remember it's there. Remember, I can *make* you eat that apple if I want to. Without me, you're just playing at childish games." She taps the apple with one thin index finger. "Now, can I go on or would you like a snack?"

"Go on," Ursula says petulantly, then adds, "I already ate."

The chief raises an eyebrow. "Bella has made the connection, along with her little journalist friend. She knows about Miracle Lake and she knows about the gold." She fixes her gaze on me. "Worse, in the last hour alone, they've managed to tell Mary's aunt and the rest of her little clutch."

My cheeks heat, hands tremble. In my pocket, I hold the vial with the antidote inside. And now they're all waiting for me to pick a side and stay there.

"Well," Mally says. "What do you have to say for yourself, *Red Queen?*"

I have to speak or I'm going to have poisoned apples shoved down my throat.

I look from the chief to Mally to Caleb to Ursula, let myself linger on James a moment, then land back on the chief.

"Legacy Loyalty," I say.

They all take turns looking at each other.

"Legacy Loyalty," James says after a minute.

"Legacy Loyalty," Ursula crows.

"Legacy Loyalty," I say again.

"Legacy Loyalty," they throw back in unison.

We all stand. We say it louder and louder and louder until we're dizzy with it.

Hellion squawks and flies around the room. Mally taps her staff on the floor so that blue sparks come out. I command the tea set to grow legs and arms, and faces this time, too, and their voices join in. The chief smiles deeply and her voice resonates under us all. James waves his hook in the air, and Ursula's dress comes to life once more as she glides from side to side on powerful tentacles.

I let myself feel this. My whole life we've been stepped on, dragged down, taken for granted. Not anymore. Now we rise. Now we stand up. Now we become what we were always meant to be, and I, for once, am going to be totally and completely free.

"LEGACY LOYALTY, LEGACY LOYALTY, LEGACY LOYALTY!" It's a frenzy now, and we're laughing. Urs and I join hands and spin, and James and I stop to kiss, and I have never been so happy.

And then we hear it coming from all around us, picking up in volume and intensity until it rises in a chant. From outside, where the sky is a blackening blanket of stars, every voice, from every ship and every member of the Legacy Army, joins us, howling and hooting in unison.

"LEGACY LOYALTY! LEGACY LOYALTY! LEGACY LOYALTY!"

It drowns out everything else.

Legacy Loyalty.

No more Bella. No more trying to stay on the right side of the law. No more trying to work within a broken system.

There is only Legacy.

Legacy Loyalty for life.

ACKNOWLEDGMENTS

MY EDITOR, JOCELYN DAVIES: WE STARTED THIS project under such different circumstances, and as the world has thrown us (and everyone) massive, unexpected challenges and blessings. I'm grateful for all the support, the laughter, the mind melds, and our common TV language. It feels like we've really been through something, you know? I love you.

To my agent at Folio Literary Management, Emily van Beek: Thank you, a million times thank you. I don't know how I would have made it through this year without you. Thank you for never faltering, for all the pictures and videos of kids and horses, and for the many gifts, physical and emotional. I love you to pieces and am yours forevermore if you'll have me.

Writing a book is always a rodeo, but doing it during a pandemic while facing health issues is another thing entirely and requires extra support. I owe many many thanks to the following people at Disney Hyperion: For their marketing efforts, Danielle DiMartino, Holly Nagel, Ian Byrne, Marina Shults, Tim Retzlaf, Dina Sherman, and Maddie Hughes; in publicity, Seale Ballenger and Lyssa Hurvitz; in sales, Monique Diman, Nicole Elmes, Lia Murphy, Michael Freeman, Loren Godfrey, Kim Knueppel, Vicki Korlishin, Meredith Lisbin, Kori Neal, and Sara Boncha; in design, Phil Buchanan,

Marci Senders, and illustrator Joshua Hixson for the amazing cover; in managing editorial Sara Liebling, Guy Cunningham, Jody Corbett, Meredith Jones, David Jaffe, and Martin Karlow; in production, Marybeth Tregarthen; and for all her help and tremendous flexibility, editorial assistant, Elanna Heda. Much gratitude to Kieran Viola for early edits as well.

Laura Ruby, Noelle Fiore, Jerelyn Elkins, and Cobey Senescu: I'm indebted to you for your generosity in terms of time, attention, and love. Thank you for checking up on me, and for sharing your experiences so openly. You're all my heroes.

Jeff Zentner, Kerry Kletter, Kathleen Glasgow, Jasmine Warga: Aside from being some of the best authors on the block, thank you for being there extra.

In the last year, I've been literally and figuratively held by the following women: Laine Overley, Linda Cannon, Kristin Moore, Mindy Laks, Johanna Debiase, Elisa Romero, Joy Romero, Yvette Montoya, Rachel Bell, Shandra vom Dorp, Samantha Samoiel, Breanna Messerole, Elizabeth LeBlanc, Sonya Feher, Sarah-Jane Drummey, Sarah McKee, Dr. Lilly Marie, Stephanie Gutz, and Amani Caraccio. You carry so much brilliance and compassion and I am lucky. Like, extra lucky.

Thanks to my wild, free-spirited, giant family, including my parents, Michel and Marie, and Dhyana and Larry; my brothers and sisters, Renee Meiffren, Celeste Meiffren-Swango, Lili Meiffren, and Gabriel Meiffren; my cousins Julia Eagleton, Mina Stone, and Alex Eagleton. Thanks also to my other-mother brothers, Eliam Kraiem and Sasha vom Dorp: You keep on showing up, and it's so cool.

To all the readers, librarians, teachers, bloggers, and especially the young people who have come to this series, I thank you and love connecting with you. I'm living my dream thanks to you. Many,

many thanks also to my students and colleagues at Taos Academy. You know how much I adore you and how hard it was to step away.

My brother Christophe Eagleton, thank you for dropping everything to be with me when I needed you most and for showing up most mornings regardless of your busy life. To my daughter, Lilu Marchasin, my son, Bodhi Marchasin, and my husband, Christopher Painter, you provide endless light and inspiration. I take every step for you, every day, all along, forever, always.